LEON M A E

To The
Stars

www.leonmaedwards.com

JOIN MY LEON M A EDWARDS CLUB

Leon M A Edwards Club members get free books, ahead of publications. So you can enjoy the book and form an opinion of how it made you feel.

Members only get emails about any promotions and when the next book is ready for receiving.

See the back of the book for details on how to sign up.

TO THE STARS

LEON M A EDWARDS

DEDICATION

I would like to dedicate this book to Andrea, Alina and Lilia for leaving me to it, to write.

ACKNOWLEDGMENTS

Thank God for giving me the confidence to start writing and the ability to write a story.

CONTENTS

1

A DAY IN MY LIFE

Autumn has turned and the clocks have gone back already. It is that time of year when it begins to get dark around quarter to four.

My name is Sarah Barns and I have the letters MSc and PhD after my name. I am thirty-two years old, five foot five, and Caucasian with a slim athletic build. I have long mousy blonde hair down to my shoulder. People would say that I have features similar to Sandra Bullock.

My personality is reserved; I am quiet and only open up to people I eventually get to know well. When I warm to people, I make funny sarcastic comments and cannot stop laughing at my own jokes and others. I have a good sense of humour and my friends and colleagues find my laugh infectious.

I think I look a tiny bit like Gwyneth Paltrow but that doesn't mean I have men falling at my feet. How I wish.

My favourite outfit is a pair of bootcut dark blue jeans, flat brown boots and a thin jumper, in which I have in various colours - light blue, maroon, green and navy blue.

For work, I wear jeans with a blouse or shirt and a short brown blazer that sits above my waistline.

In my spare time, I like outdoor runs and going to the gym for fitness and staying healthy.

I have been single for my entire life. Anyone I make friends with puts me in the friendship box before I even get a chance. I have fancied a lot of guys in the past but never quite managed to start a relationship. They see me as their sister. I tried internet dating but I kept showing interest in the wrong kind of guy and so gave up.

I am an only child as my parents only wanted one.

I have not done much with my life as I chose to put that on hold and focus on my education. For example, stepping into the big wide world, I concentrated on forging a career in teaching Astrophysics at Oxford University. I think I am at a point now where I can focus on my personal life. I can finally start to live.

I have never travelled abroad due to focusing on my education, as well as being penniless as a student. Now I have my rent, travel costs, student loan and household bills to pay before I can consider paying for a holiday abroad. I have always wanted to go to North America. There is nothing else that I would like to do.

I LIVE IN MILTON KEYNES, in an area called 'The Hub', in a block of apartments above restaurants and bars. The restaurants provide a range of cuisine, from pizza and fish and chips to Indian, Chinese and even Caribbean food, but I prefer to cook for myself rather than run out of money eating a different country each night.

The 'Hub' is a square area with entrances on each corner. In the centre of the square is a concealed water feature with small steel-rimmed holes lying flush with the concrete. Water is pumped from underground and jets of water spout from the holes. They jump out three at a time and curve inwards as high as four feet. The feature only works in the summer if it is a warm sunny day.

Thursday, Friday and Saturday nights can be a little rowdy but being high up on the tenth floor with double glazing drowns out the noise.

My apartment has a short hallway that leads to a pokey kitchen on the left and two bedrooms on the right. Opposite the bedrooms is a small bathroom with a bath with a shower inside. At the end of the hallway is the living room where my window faces the square. The living room is big enough to house a dining table and two chairs, a three-seater sofa and a coffee table in front on a rug.

I have lived in Milton Keynes all my life. I grew up in 'Shenley Lodge' and my parents still live there. I went away to study at University and came back with no plans.

I STUDIED astrology because I am fascinated with space and the stars. I believe that other beings are out there in the galaxy. I also believe that there is some kind of god out there because the theory of the Big Bang is just that; a theory. Something must have been the cause – it didn't just magically happen.

. . .

I HAVE a PhD in Physics and when I came back to MK, I applied to teach at Oxford University. I didn't think I would get the job because I didn't go to a private school or get my degree there.

They have a Physics department and, specifically, a sub-department in Astrophysics. The course allows me to passionately talk about how the universe came about and how many planets we know exist. This is probably the reason why I do not have a boyfriend as I would talk him to death on this subject!

My interview took place in front of a panel of three senior academic lecturers and a representative from HR. I was nervous, as I had not expected to even be granted an interview, but I have now been working here for five years. I am responsible for organising my own method of delivering the syllabus and I both lecture and hold classes.

I thought I would find it hard to stand up in front of highly intelligent students and wondered if the students would correct my teaching. I had even worried that I would get my PowerPoint slides the wrong way round. However, after a few weeks, it became easier and more comfortable standing in front of one hundred and eighty-one pupils.

I HAVE SPENT my whole life on my education and career, firstly telling myself that a college diploma would be good enough for me. Then I told myself that a university degree would give me satisfaction. After I achieved that, I thought a master's degree would be enough for me but that did not satisfy me. So, I thought a PhD would be enough, but that did not fulfil me either. Now, despite being a University lecturer, I still do not feel totally complete.

In the past, I have tried to rack my brain to work out what is missing in my life. Is it travelling, being in a relationship, or are there other challenges I want to achieve? For now, I have my job and my own place, even though it's rented and not far from my parents.

However, I envy five friends who I am close to. They are in relationships and fulfilled. I am not jealous of their relationships, but I do envy them finding their happiness.

ON WEEKDAYS, my alarm wakes me at six o'clock. I leave my apartment by seven o'clock. I drive towards the A421 that leads to the A43 and, eventually, the M40 motorway. I stay on the M40 for one junction to join the A34 at junction nine. I travel along the A34 until I come off the slip road for the A44, which takes me along minor roads, to eventually reach Haldane Road. At the end of the road is a parking area.

I arrive about half-past eight and don't start my lectures until ten o'clock, so, I go to a well-known coffee shop, about a ten-minute walk from my office.

I have a medium latte and an almond croissant. I take my time, staying there for about forty-five minutes. Once I have finished my coffee, I head back to the university, pick up my lecture work from my office, then head to my first lecture.

I have a tiny office the size of a shoebox. I check what subject and topic I will be lecturing for the day and prepare my PowerPoint slides ten minutes before the lecture begins at ten o'clock.

I have my lunch at one o'clock when I go with a work colleague to the same pub in town.

After lunch, we rush back for lectures which start at two-thirty. When I finish at five o'clock, I go straight home, via the A34, without stopping for anything. There are three ways of getting to work and back but I like to use the same route every day.

During the week, my evenings consist of eating dinner and having a glass of red wine. I am usually too tired to cook from scratch, so I have a microwave dinner. If I do not have work to take home, I will watch my favourite soaps to make the evenings fly by. If I have time, I will go for a short run around the block.

Weekends are spent washing the clothes I have worn for the week and hanging them on clothes racks in my living room and bathroom. I then get some errands done, like shopping, getting my car serviced and fuelled up, sorting out the post and any other business. I can get most of my shopping at the local supermarket which is quite nearby, so apart from sorting out the car, I don't need to drive.

I VISIT my parents once a month, on a Sunday for a roast, so they can see that I am healthy and alive. I make a habit of seeing them on the last Sunday of the month, so I do not need to work out in my head when to see them.

I go to the gym on Saturday and Sunday nights as I do not have a social life, then, come Monday, life starts all over again.

I HAVE four genuine close friends who I do not get a chance to see often due to their family life. I have known them since school and college. I am also close to a work colleague who has been a friend since I began at the university. She also has a family and I only see her at lunchtime when we go to a local pub.

I do not have a social life, which is why I go for runs and attend the gym. I have been recommended to join a social club but that is not actually for me as I am content with my own company.

I see my four friends roughly every three months when one of them will arrange a night out at the weekend. I leave it to them because they are better at organising the date than I am.

My friends are Natalie Lamb, Georgina Wells, Kerry Mason and Mercedes Hunjan. My friend at work is Belinda Jenkin.

NATALIE IS MARRIED to her university sweetheart, with two children aged four and six. She is Caucasian with shoulder-length brown hair and a slim build. She is five foot nine inches tall. She is thirty-one years of age.

She tends to wear a pair of jeans with a T-shirt and a hoody, and a pair of pumps on her feet,

She is always smiley, upbeat, easy to talk to and the life and soul of the party. She always has an ear to lend if you are going through problems. If I had an issue, she would be my first point of call. She mostly instigates a night out and arranges where to meet.

Her husband is quite reserved and I wonder how they met as they seem opposite to each other? But he is great with the kids and keeps her feet on the ground. She will come up with hair-raising ideas and he will rein her in.

She is an intelligent woman, a Corporate Banker in London, employed at a merchant bank. She deals with the financial affairs of medium to large corporate companies, such as loans, mergers and acquisitions.

GEORGINA IS in a long-term relationship with her girlfriend. She is Asian with long black hair and has an athletic build. She is five foot six inches tall and aged thirty-three.

Her choice of fashion is a pair of trousers and a striped shirt with a thin tank top. The shoes she tends to wear are plimsols.

Her personality is placid; it is difficult to enrage her and she has a calming effect on people.

She met her girlfriend through a dating website that catered for both mixed and same-sex people. She is engaged to a beautiful black girl who is a couple of years older than her. They have been together for a couple of years.

Georgina works as a manager for a mobile communication company. She has to travel to Newbury for work, which takes her a little over an hour.

It is quite sad as she and her partner are struggling to have a baby. They cannot find a surrogate who would carry the child.

KERRY HAS TWO CHILDREN, aged three and one, with her long-term partner. They are not married or engaged. They are content and do not feel it neces-sary to tie the knot.

She is a size thirteen after having two children and enjoying her food. She is Caucasian with blonde hair down to her shoulder and her face is slightly filled out. She is thirty-five years of age.

Because of her work, she wears jeans, pullovers and waterproof walking shoes for both work and personal life.

Her personality is free-spirited and she can be a bit scatter-brained. She does not conform to a daily routine and so she juggles with family life. When having a conversation, she can waffle a lot about what is happening in her life. It can be hard to keep her on track with topical conversations and talk about what is happening in your own life, however, she will be there for you physically if you need a shoulder to lean on.

Kerry works as an Agricultural Manager, which involves taking care of a farm. Her duties include administration, budgeting and hiring of staff. You would think that she would be organised at home considering what she does for a living.

MERCEDES IS ALSO married but with no kids. She has been struggling to fall pregnant and both Mercedes and her husband have been struggling to come to terms with the thought of not having a family.

She is Indian with silky black hair that falls to the base of her neck and she wears it in a ponytail. She is very slim and petite at only five foot four inches. She is naturally beautiful with a flawless complexion. She is thirty-two years of age.

Her personality is bubbly and she has an optimistic view on life. She has not one bad bone in her body, much like the rest of us. I know that she is struggling with not being able to have her own children, however, she masks the hurt inside quite well with her sparkling upbeat mood.

She is a Recruitment Consultant in the medical profession. She focuses on recruiting for specialist consultants and surgeons.

BELINDA IS MARRIED with three children aged two, five and eight. She is Chinese and wears her natural black hair dyed maroon. She wears her hair tied up at the back. She has a pear-shaped frame and is a size sixteen. Her face has some blemishes but she is still extremely pretty. She is five foot nine inches and so she carries her frame well. She is thirty-nine years of age.

Her personality is similar to Kerry where she can get carried away talking about her life, forgetting to ask about yours, yet she is a good listener and is always able to give you advice. She is open and not opinionated.

She is a lecturer herself but she is at a senior level and so gets involved in course coordination and updating course syllabuses. She is my supervisor but she does not behave like she is. We go for lunch together every working day.

She always has some form of engagement at the weekends whether it is seeing family or going away. I always hear about it on Monday.

FINALLY, my parents. They are in their sixties now and both still work. They cannot afford to retire early, so must continue until they reach retirement age.

My mum works as a nurse and my dad is a car mechanic for an independent garage. He always had the dream of running his own workshop but that never materialised.

Mum is quiet and reserved. She is very approachable if I need a mother/daughter talk. We are the same height and she has a slight waistline due to her age. She adores my dad and they still do romantic things together which makes me want to have a relationship.

My dad's personality is similar to my mum's which is probably why they get on so well. They met while going to dancing lessons. My dad swears that he went there to impress someone other than mum. He never told me who that was. My mum claims that the teacher always coupled them up and naturally they fell for each other. I roll my eyes every time they tell me that story.

Dad is taller than my mum at six foot six. He has a solid frame but through years of standing under a car, he has a slight hunch. He is still able to do his job; he simply has to focus on less physical work.

My parents' names are George and Terrie.

2

NO REGRETS

It is Thursday today and this week has dragged. A couple of days ago, I received a text, out of the blue, about a last-minute arrangement to go out tonight. Luckily, I have a clear schedule this week. It is not like I have a heavy social life, so, I welcome the invite. I am going out for a catch up with some girlfriends I last saw about four months ago.

HUSBANDS, fiancés and partners are not allowed, not that I have a partner myself to leave at home. Being the only one without someone in my life does make me feel small. I find myself being reminded of this when I hear about how their lives are going.

IT IS NOW my first lecture for the day and I am teaching the probability of other life forms. I find this my favourite topic as I do not know what will come out of my students' mouths.

I have a full lecture hall and I was five minutes into my teaching.

I asked my students to answer the question – What purpose do we have on Earth?

One of the students in the front row puts his hand up and says, 'I don't think there is a purpose.'

I have no opinion on his belief but want him to elaborate. 'Can you go into detail a bit more?'

The same student hesitates, 'I... believe that we only exist. No one has told us why we are here. We have not been told our purpose here.'

I question his hypothesis; 'So, why do you think we have not been told our reason for being here?'

The student has a perplexed expression. 'I think it is the evolution of life. The galaxy is revolving. We are the current evolution.'

I think about his answer and play devil's advocate; 'Do you not believe that there are other humans out there. That they have been told their purpose?'

The student thinks about my question before replying, 'No. If there were other humans, why would they be living so far apart from us? Why have we not had anyone visit us? Also why would they be told their purpose and not us?'

I suggest a reason; 'They have the same technology as us and so they cannot travel the distance like us. Why assume that another species has more technological advancement?'

A second student at the back asks, 'What do you believe?'

I am open with them and say, 'I think that it would be an awful waste of space if we are the only people in the universe. Don't you think? I believe we have to figure out our own purpose. It is not for us to wait to be told our purpose. Something must have caused our existence. We didn't instantly appear.'

A third student voices her opinion; 'Would you want to go into space? Travel to the ends of the galaxy to see what other beings are there? Find out if they have worked out their purpose?'

I have been thinking about that all my life, so I reply, 'Yes, I would. If I could leave this planet, even with no possibility of returning, I would do it and somehow send a message that could travel back to Earth.'

The same female student asks me another question; 'What would you tell them about Earth?'

I like her question, 'That is a good question. I would tell them that we work, walk and run for leisure and we have cars. I would tell them that we have sex for pleasure as well as to procreate. That we... find love and live on money.'

The first student at the front asks an interesting question; 'What would you ask about them?'

I think that is another good question! 'I would ask if they know of other planets, if they have had wars and if they have a similar financial structure.'

Before we know it, the lecture has finished.

WHILE I GO to my next lecture session, I ponder on what my students asked me. I wonder what it would be like to go up into space. There are companies that now provide a trip into space for about half an hour before coming back to Earth.

I wish I had the money to go.

My next lecture is on the theory of time travel and folding space to get from A to B.

AFTER MY SECOND LECTURE, I head for lunch with Belinda. We go to 'The Lamb and Flag' pub. It is about a ten-minute walk, so it is easier than trying to find a parking space.

HER FAMILY IS ORIGINALLY from China and she was born here. She wears thin black-rimmed glasses and appears authoritative in her field. Our conversations over lunch are about work and our lives. She finds it hard to talk about mundane things or gossip from television or magazines.

She always asks me what is happening in my life and I never have anything of interest to say, so she carries the conversation for the majority of the time.

THE PUB INTERIOR contains a lovely varnished light brown oak bar and beams in the walls. It is a gastropub rather than a man's drinking pub.

The menu consists of steak and burgers, all served with salad or fries, steak and ale pie with peas and gravy, and a variety of wraps.

The barman knows our faces because we come in here every weekday. He knows what drinks we have every time.

We sit at whatever table is available, rather than booking ahead. Our choice of meals does not vary that much as the quality of the food is always good and I find the meals so filling that I don't need a big meal in the evening.

WE HAVE ALREADY ORDERED our food and, while we wait, we make conversation.

Belinda puts her elbows on the table and rests her chin on the back of her hands, 'What have you been up to?'

I cross my arms on the table and lean forward, 'What has happened? I can't think of anything.'

Belinda is more direct and demands, 'Are you seeing anyone now?'

I wish I were, 'No. I can't seem to find anyone who is single and not into one-night stands.'

Belinda stares at me with a woeful expression, 'I don't get it. You are attractive, what men go for. I don't get what you are doing wrong. Are you actually looking?'

I think back to what I have done already, 'I told you that I tried internet dating. It either didn't go beyond the first date or they hinted that they wanted an FB. Of course, I am not into having a partner simply for sex. Besides, the students are all too young and every staff member I work with is either married or in a long-term relationship.'

Belinda ponders as she stares into space, 'Why don't you join a social group or dance class like salsa, or a running club? Something where you will meet normal men and have something in common.'

The thought of that puts me off; 'That is not really me. I would rather be patient and believe that someone will eventually come into my life.'

Belinda expresses disappointment in my attitude; 'Your career is sorted, you have no other ambitions to achieve, so, it's time to focus on your personal life now. Not a year, two years or five years away; now! Time is too short to be dilly-dallying about.'

I sigh at her with a smile. 'I have all the time in the world. If it is meant to be, it will happen.'

Belinda accepts my response and changes the subject to the weekend.

All I can talk about is tonight; 'I am going out with some college mates tonight. Apart from that, I have nothing on.'

Belinda groans and says, 'I have to go and see the in-laws. He insists and so we are going to Wales.'

I feel jealous. 'I wish I had in-laws to see. My weekend consists of gym, washing and shopping.'

Belinda wishes her life was like mine; 'I would swap my weekend for yours anytime. No kids, no husband to clean behind. Ah, bliss.'

I prefer her life; 'Kids to make the weeks go by quickly. Waking up next to someone every day. Weekends to fill. I want your life.'

Our food eventually arrives and we tuck in. We hardly say anything to each other as we enjoy our steak and ale pie and chips.

After we finish eating and drink our Coke and lemonade, Belinda asks where I am going tonight.

After I finish swallowing my mouthful of lemonade, I tell her what is happening. 'I am going to a place called 'Revolution'. We are meeting outside. I will probably get there earlier and get a bite to eat before they get there. There are a few places to eat. Saves cooking another microwave meal.'

Belinda laughs, 'You eat microwave meals? Why don't you cook something more nutritious?'

The thought puts me off; 'Spend a whole evening cooking and it is only me eating it? That reminds me too much of being single. Besides, it is quicker to microwave.'

Belinda comes across as overwhelmed; 'I cannot believe you are still single. I don't get it. You're smart, well-educated and you have no baggage. I don't get it.'

I agree with her; 'I know. I look at certain women and wonder how come they have a boyfriend when they are mouthy, rude and make no effort with themselves?'

I cannot stop thinking about a woman called Julie. 'What is with Julie? Every time there is a faculty meeting, she gives me daggers. What is that about?'

Belinda does not see it that way. 'She has not met you yet. She has spoken to everyone else, including me, so, she is probably just curious why you haven't introduced yourself yet.'

I think about her comment, 'Nah. One time, in her first week, she asked me for directions. I happily walked her to her classroom. I made conversation with her. I even suggested lunch one day. She didn't take up my offer.'

Belinda shrugs her shoulders; 'I don't know. Maybe you offended her somehow. She gets on with everyone else. Maybe she hates you.'

I give her a fake laugh as she finds her comment amusing. 'She has been here six months now. I think I will have it out with her the next time we meet.'

We pay for the meals and start walking back to work. On our way back, Belinda quizzes me on my personal life.

Belinda is coy as she asks, 'Have you ever slept with anyone?'

I feel embarrassed; 'What makes you ask?'

Belinda asks, 'Have you ever been abroad?'

I find that question less embarrassing; 'No. There's never been the right time.'

Belinda asks me a third question; 'Have you ever been in love?'

Another straightforward question; 'No.'

Belinda stops in her tracks and asks, 'What have you done with your life, Sarah?'

I stand there, thinking, 'I guess I have done nothing. I spent my whole life concentrating on my studies. And now, I focus on my work.'

Belinda is surprised as she smiles and continues walking. Nothing else is mentioned and I do not think any more about her questions.

When we get back, we go our separate ways and I prepare for my next lecture.

I AM in my office inspecting the lecture notes that I will be presenting on PowerPoint. While I go through my notes, I cannot help pondering on Belinda's questions. They have made me evaluate my life and observe what I have achieved.

I realise I have done nothing. I have never kissed a boy, made love, travelled abroad or been drunk.

The thoughts have made me feel a little depressed, realising that I have not done a lot with my life. It makes me wonder when I will make time for those things to happen.

I look at my routine and realise if I do not change anything, I will still be doing the same things twenty years from now!

The problem is, how do I go from focusing on work to starting to live my life outside of work? My friends are settled down so I cannot instantly pick up the phone to ask what they are up to this weekend. The thought of being by myself going out to singles' bars fills me with dread.

I have no one to go on holiday with and I find the thought of going by myself daunting.

Wow! Is that the time? I have to get going to my next lecture. I will mull over in my head how I can start doing some living.

3

FIRST TIME FOR EVERYTHING

When I finish work, I put everything away and switch off the computer. I am still mulling over what I can do to improve my life.

I am excited about going out tonight with my girlfriends as I have not been out in months. I will make sure I get drunk and experience what that is like for the first time. Hopefully, the effects of the alcohol will give me the confidence to snog someone for the first time.

WHILE I AM DRIVING along the A34, I predict that I will be home by half-past six as per usual with the traffic snarling up three miles from junction nine of the M40.

Even though I should not be doing this, in between crawling at five miles an hour and being at a standstill, I text my girlie friends to confirm where we are going to meet up and at what time.

My college friends text back to tell me that we are going straight to 'Revolution' for eight o'clock, to allow time for everyone to get home, have dinner and get ready.

WHEN I GET HOME, I take the post from the letterbox and place it on top of the cupboard, then I go for a shower, during which I think of what food to eat before meeting up with the girls.

There are a few fast food outlets and restaurants where I can grab a wrap or a sandwich that will tide me over, so I decide on a 'Subway' sandwich.

I am getting excited about going out and letting my hair down. I want to make sure I get drunk tonight. It will be interesting to find out what it is like to lose control of myself. I have no idea if I will like any alcohol.

After I get out of the shower, I go to my wardrobe to see if I have a nice dress to wear. I want to make an effort. I have a few formal dresses in purple, red, black and green. I decide to wear the green dress. It is a plain, knee-length dress with a curved neckline, which covers what boobs I don't have.

I now have to decide what shoes will go with the dress. I am sure I have a pair of green high-heel shoes I bought to go with the dress, but I cannot find them, so settle on the next best thing – a pair of black heels with black tights to complete the outfit.

Once I am ready to go, I bring up a taxi app on my mobile. The app allows me to book a taxi and pay for it. I enter the time I want to be picked up which is half-past seven. Once I book the taxi, I can monitor the taxi's journey to see if it is on time.

I take the lift to get to street level and wait on the pavement for the taxi. It arrives on time and I tell the driver to take me to 'Subway'.

WHEN I GET TO 'SUBWAY', I order a tuna mayonnaise with salad and black pepper. I also have a white coffee. I have twenty minutes to eat my sandwich and drink my coffee.

I start to dwell again on what Belinda said about me doing nothing with my life. At least I will start tonight by getting extremely drunk. I will try every type of spirit except for whisky.

I am excited about seeing my friends from college; Natalie, Georgina, Kerry and Mercedes.

WE MET at Milton Keynes College. We spent a lot of time together socialising outside of college. I didn't drink, though, as I did not feel the need to get drunk. So, I was always the designated driver.

I think staying sober made it extremely hard to try to meet anyone. My friends met their other halves through getting drunk and the men cracking on to them.

Thinking back, I wish I could have been like them as I would have probably been married with kids by now.

But at the same time, I would not have been able to achieve so much academically if I were in a relationship. I preferred to focus on making sure I achieved my doctorate, so I spent every waking moment studying and let my social life fall by the wayside.

. . .

I HAVE no regrets over the choices I made to get to where I am now. I knew it would not be fair to try to have a relationship, yet putting my studies first. I couldn't put a guy through that. I would have resented the man for coming before my education or making me give up on my PhD, so it was so much easier to stay single.

BELINDA'S QUESTIONS have made me think - I have reached the end of my studies and I have no other ambitions or goals I want to achieve in my career, so where do I go from here? The thought of staring at my four walls for the next twenty years freaks me out. I don't want to be the only person single and with no kids.

The thought of seeing myself continuing to trudge through work, lecture, lunch, lecture, home and then eating a microwave meal, that scares me and I want to make sure that does not happen.

The only way I can change my future is to change my life today. I have to get drunk tonight and try to find enough Dutch courage to chat a man up.

I have no idea how to chat a man up. I wouldn't know where to start.

When I finally finish my sandwich and gulp the remaining coffee, it is about that time to meet up with my friends.

WHEN I GET to the entrance of 'Revolution', I see Natalie, Georgina, Kerry and Mercedes are here already and I am the last to arrive. I could have eaten dinner faster, but I assumed I would be too early. I notice there is an additional person in our group who I have not met before. She is standing with Kerry, so I presume she came with her. I have to find out who she is.

I can see everyone has already initially caught up with each other. They all gravitate towards me and simultaneously ask me what is new in my life.

I tell them that nothing interesting has happened. We all go inside and go straight to the bar. I have no idea what alcohol to try first. I ask Kerry which drink tastes nice and how strong it is. Afterwards, I ask who her friend is. She tells me that it is someone from work and she is new in town, which is why she had invited her.

I go up to her to say hi and introduce myself properly. Her name is Amber and she gives me a brief smile and acts nervous around me before walking off. I wonder if I have offended her somehow. I instinctively shrug it off.

Kerry passes me a shot and glass of wine. I down the shot thinking that is how everyone does it. She tells me to go easy and drink a glass of wine first to pace myself. I have no idea what wine to have and let Kerry choose for me.

Natalie stops me from ordering and suggests that we put ten pounds each into a kitty. She takes the kitty and orders the first drinks, but Georgina interrupts and says that she only wants a lemonade as it is a school night.

We then find a high table to stand around and properly talk about what has happened in each of our lives. I stay quiet and let the others decide amongst themselves who wants to talk first.

Georgina is happy to start and says, 'Well, I have some news to tell. We are getting married.'

Natalie, Kerry and I are happy for her and wonder why she did not want a glass of wine. I notice that Mercedes is quiet and appears withdrawn But I don't think the others have noticed. I do not expect Georgina to notice as she has her good news to be happy about. I will ask her what is up later.

When we all calm down from the exciting news, Natalie shares her good news; 'There is something that I have to share. I have been given a chance to buy into the firm. It means getting a loan, but I will be a partner. It means a share of the profits as well as a salary.'

Kerry, Georgina and I are all happy about this second piece of good news. By the time we finish hearing their stories, we have finished our first glass of wine. Mercedes is still struggling to join in the celebrations. The other girls have still not noticed her being withdrawn.

For the second round, Natalie orders vodka and Coke. I am keen to find out what it tastes like.

When Natalie returns with the drinks, it is Kerry's turn to share good news; 'I have some news as well. Remember when I mentioned that we were trying to get an extension to make the house a four-bed home? Well, after two years of going back and forth with the council, they eventually gave us the planning permission.'

They ask Mercedes and I if we have any news to tell and we both disappointingly say no.

AN HOUR INTO THE NIGHT, we are now on 'Jaeger Bombs' which I do not like, but I decide to go along with it. I wish I was pregnant now, to avoid having to drink this stuff. I take the whole shot in my mouth and hold it before plucking up the courage to swallow it in one. I wince from the aftertaste and hope she does not order another round.

My head is fuzzy now after what I think is five drinks. We've already had two glasses of wine, a vodka and Coke and strawberry gin!

I thought I would feel out of control and want to cause a fight, but I feel sleepy and want to find a corner to rest my eyes. I am not having that feeling of the room spinning that I have heard about.

Natalie, Kerry and Georgina are dancing and Mercedes and I are standing by our table and making sure our belongings are safe. Even though I feel woozy, I still have my wits about me and I want to know why Mercedes has been distant so far.

I think of a way to ask the question; 'You seem distant tonight. Is everything okay?'

Mercedes struggles to smile and shrug off the question; 'It's nothing.'

I know that something is up and so I push her to tell me, 'It's okay. This is what friends are for. What is it?'

Mercedes appears upset now as she eventually tells me, 'Don't get me wrong, I am really happy for Georgina, but it made it real for me. I am not able to have children.'

I find myself sobering up quite quickly, 'Have you tried every avenue?'

Mercedes has a distance behind her eyes. 'We already looked at my egg count and it is too low for IVF.'

'WHAT ABOUT YOUR HUSBAND? Is his sperm count okay?'

Mercedes wipes her eyes and continues, 'Simon has a low count himself and this is why we were told that IVF on the NHS would not be viable. We do not have ten thousand pounds to spend on private IVF. Hearing Georgina's news brought it home.'

I feel for her as she has been dreaming of having a family since I can remember. She wanted to start a family as soon as they were married. I wish I could do something about it.

TWENTY MINUTES LATER, the girls come back from dancing and more drinks are ordered, this time green-coloured shots and a vodka and Coke.

We all down the shots together and, surprisingly, I like the flavour and it is not harsh on the throat. We notice that there is an empty table across the room so we sit down. We start to talk about what this place is like and what the men are like here. We are basically talking nonsense as a result of the alcohol.

Mercedes and I glance at each other; she has asked me not to say anything to the others so I promise that I will not.

Georgina and Kerry reckon I am drunk enough to chat up a guy. My mind is still coherent and I still have my faculties, even though I have the sensation of being drunk. I still do not feel confident, but they push me to approach a guy on the dance floor.

I tell Georgina and Kerry that I need another shot to try to loosen myself so I can have the confidence to go up to a guy.

Natalie gets me a drink that will do the trick. She comes back with a green-coloured drink and tells me that it is a 'Frog Hopper'. It appears slimy as I take a gulp, but I like the flavour.

I think the cocktail did the trick and I am ready to try and snog someone.

. . .

I HAVE to focus on walking in a straight line as I approach the edge of the dance floor. I do not realise that there are a couple of steps and almost trip down but grab a pillar next to me. I giggle to myself as I feel embarrassed that someone could have seen me. Once I get my balance back, I scan the dance floor for someone my age who is attractive.

I spot a man wearing blue bootcut jeans with a labelled pink shirt. He is about six feet tall with dark brown hair and is Caucasian. He has similar features to Hugh Grant. I discreetly start dancing towards him with my side to him, so I am not too obvious.

I pretend to bump into him by mistake to get his attention; he acknowledges me and apologises, thinking he walked into me. I smile at him to get a reaction. When he smiles back, I rub my back against him, assuming he will respond. He starts to gently gyrate the front of his body against my back but does not use his hands to take hold of me.

I find his hands and encourage him to put them around my torso as I rub my bum against his crotch. I have no idea what I am doing, I'm just going by what I have seen in films like 'Dirty Dancing'. I feel that I am being quite sexy but have no idea if I am making a fool of myself.

I turn round to face him as I sway my hips from side to side, hoping for a peck on the lips. I awkwardly make a pass at his mouth as I close my eyes. I make a quick peck on his lip thinking that is how you kiss someone. I open my eyes and realise he finds my failed attempt at making a pass quite amusing. He holds my face and makes a slow move towards my lips. I patiently wait for him to come in for a kiss. He gazes into my eyes and our lips naturally gravitate towards one another. I feel like we are the only two on the dance floor.

He presses his lips against mine and holds them there as I reciprocate. He then slowly slips a tip of his tongue in my mouth and I find it odd. This is the first time I am experiencing kissing properly compared to junior school. I open my mouth slightly as I allow him to continue putting his tongue in my mouth. I find his kisses exciting and cannot believe that I have pulled a man while being drunk for the first time.

SARAH'S FRIENDS express shock as they watch their best friend having a snog for the first time since they have known her. They cheer her on as she is engrossed on the dance floor. Natalie manages a smile as she gets into the mood.

I CAN HEAR my friends rooting for me as we pull away from our clinch. We continue dancing together, gazing into each other's eyes as we struggle not to smile at each other, laughing about this situation.

.   .   .

EVENTUALLY, I shout in his ear to ask what his name is. He tells me it is Ben Hawk and asks what my name is. After I tell him my name, I tell him that this is not what I normally do and that it is the first time I have ever been drunk. I explain that I have spent my whole life on my academic career and feel it is time to focus on letting my hair down. I almost scared him off by saying settling down with someone.

He finds me funny and tells me that cannot believe that I have never been out drinking. We find out that we both live within a couple of miles of Milton Keynes' centre. We find out that we went to the same school but we do not remember ever seeing each other there.

I discover that he works in a bank as an Accounts Manager and he is impressed that I work at Oxford University. We continue chatting until my friends are ready to go home.

We both naturally ask for each other's number and enter them into our mobile phones. We text each other to make sure we entered the numbers correctly.

Then my friends pull at my arm to go with them. I really want to stay with him and apologise for their abruptness.

4

RE-EVALUATE MY LIFE

It is close to one o'clock in the morning when we leave; knowing that they stay open until two-thirty, we agree to go round to the local kebab van a couple of minutes' walk from here.

The air hits me and I am completely out of it from the amount of alcohol I have consumed. I find myself struggling to walk in a straight line and have to grab hold of Natalie's arm. Natalie finds it amusing seeing me drunk for the first time in her life.

The four of us all have the same choice of kebab, but the pitta is so overloaded, we cannot control the food dropping on the pavement as we tuck into them.

While we are eating by the van, they start asking me about the man I met. I tell them that all I know is his name and what he does for a living and that we have exchanged numbers. I also remember to tell them that, apparently, we went to the same school together.

AFTER WE HAVE FINISHED EATING, we decide to flag down two taxis to share between us to get home. I left it to the girls to sort out finding two taxis as I am completely out of it. While I wait for them to find us taxis, it is getting cold and I start to crave my own bed.

After five minutes of struggling to find a taxi nearby, I quickly tell them that I have my app, but they will have to book it as I am too drunk to focus on a small screen. I give it to Natalie to book our two taxis, then she tells me it will be here in ten minutes.

Feeling the chill in the night air and thinking of my bed makes ten minutes feel like half an hour. My feet are killing me in my high heel shoes and the balls of my feet are numb now.

I now feel sick after having that kebab and want to get home right away. I ask Natalie to check my phone to see how much time has passed since we last checked. Natalie tells me that only two minutes have passed but it feels like five.

Eventually, our taxis arrive and we say goodbye to each other. I speak to Mercedes quietly, telling her that she can speak to me any time about her bad news. She appreciates my discretion.

I GO in the taxi with Natalie, while Georgina, Kerry and Mercedes go in the other taxi. Natalie and I live close together while the other three live not far from each other.

The journey makes me feel queasy and I pray that I do not get sick in the car. I know that I will be sick as soon as I get back home.

I GET DROPPED off first and I hug Natalie in the car before getting out. I give her some money towards the fare and the taxi drives away.

I get to the lift and press the button frantically as I do not want to be sick here. It eventually arrives and I quickly get in and press the button for my floor. I swear the lift is moving slower than normal.

After several attempts at getting the key in the keyhole, I finally get inside the flat.

I GO into the bathroom and kneel beside the toilet, but nothing comes up, so I go into the bedroom and sit at the end of the bed.

Yep, the room is spinning. I lie on my back and close my eyes, thinking that this will block out the feeling, but it makes it worse.

I do not move and patiently wait for the spinning to stop. I find myself falling asleep upright on the edge of my bed.

When I open my eyes, I find myself over the toilet bowl again and have no idea how I got here. I suddenly start to hurl and watch tonight's consumption go down the toilet. I do not enjoy this feeling and notice my eyes tearing up from the retching. I feel like I am going to die right here.

I will never, ever drink again. I now know why I never drank in the first place. From the number of times I had seen Natalie, Kerry, Georgina and Mercedes throwing up, I should have known better.

I think I have been here for half an hour or an hour. I wait for a few seconds to see if anything is going to come up again. Nothing does. I must have emptied everything from my stomach. I will give brushing my teeth a miss. I am happy to go to sleep with the taste of vomit in my mouth.

WHEN I GET BACK to bed and close my eyes, the room is not spinning anymore.

NEXT DAY, I phone in sick and blame it on food poisoning. I get paranoid that I told Belinda I was going out last night to get drunk. I hope my boss does not mention my absence to her and she gets me in trouble.

I still feel like throwing up, I have a throbbing headache and a horrible aftertaste in my mouth. I cannot get out of bed as I feel too weak to move. Now I know what it is like to be drunk but I regret finding out the hard way.

My stomach feels like I have food poisoning as it is in knots. I also have indigestion which I blame on the amount of alcohol I drank. I decide to stay in bed and allow the awful feelings to subside.

IT IS the afternoon and I am still feeling at death's door. I finally force myself out of bed to get some headache tablets. My stomach is still aching as well, so I am hoping the painkillers will deal with both.

I try to swallow the tablet with water at first but it feels like a swallowing a piece of Lego. It makes me gag as I cringe trying to force it down my throat with plenty of water. I end up dissolving the tablet in the glass of water. Once the fizzy water calms down, I try to drink but still feel sick when I try. My throat feels sore and dry. I end up taking small sips and take about twenty minutes finishing it.

IT IS NOW the evening and I still feel the same as I felt this morning. I try watching television with a blanket over me. I struggle to focus on what is happening in the programme as my head is fuzzy. I also start to doze despite trying to keep my eyes open.

I am glad it is Saturday tomorrow and so I do not need to worry about work.

IT IS close to nine o'clock now and I cannot stay up any longer. I still have a slight headache despite the painkillers. My tummy still feels a bit queasy. It must have been the kebab I had. I wonder if my friends have felt the same symptoms as me because we all ate the same.

. . .

DURING THE NIGHT, I get up and rush to the toilet trying to be sick but I have nothing in my stomach. I have not had anything to eat all day due to lack of appetite. I have only drunk water to try and rehydrate myself.

I HAVE an inkling that I have food poisoning, thanks to the kebab meat. It cannot be the 'Subway' as I had tuna. Also, 'Subway' has a proper kitchen and five-star hygiene standards, not that I am saying kebab vans do not have food standards.

IT IS NOW Saturday morning and I have had broken sleep due to running to the bathroom regularly.

My hangover is beginning to subside but my tummy still does not feel right. I still put it down to the alcohol as it is the first time I have been drunk.

IT IS NOW Sunday and I am totally back to normal and able to have a proper meal without feeling sick. I have no more hangover and my tummy is fine.

I get my usual microwave meal out and put it in the oven to heat up. I feel I have not eaten for a week and cannot eat this lasagne meal fast enough. I find myself gulping a glass of squash after every two or three mouthfuls.

A few hours later, my tummy feels queasy again and I find myself throwing up. The microwave meal had been in date. I only drink fluid for the rest of the day to ride out the nausea.

I lie on the sofa for the rest of the afternoon and watch rubbish television while drifting in and out of sleep. I hope that I will be fine for work tomorrow.

By the time I am ready for bed at ten o'clock, I feel a lot better, even though I still have a fuzzy head.

IT IS NOW Monday and I am still not one hundred percent. However, I do not want to get behind on my student markings or miss any more lectures.

For some reason, my stomach still feels a bit tender and wonder if I have had food poisoning.

I will text Mercedes to ask her advice on what I should have experienced when having a hangover. Something did not feel right.

MY DAY at work is as per usual, including meeting up with Belinda for lunch. Once we are sat down waiting for our food, I wait for Belinda to bring up my absence on Friday. I have never taken a day off work as a result of over-indulgence. I feel like I have betrayed my beliefs. I do not want Belinda to think I will be making a habit of it. I wonder if she thinks that I phoned in sick because of Thursday night.

During lunch, we talk about how her weekend was with her in-laws in Wales. She tells me that she found it challenging but her kids enjoyed themselves.

BELINDA ASKS how Thursday night went and I hesitantly tell her that I drank too much. I also tell her that I met Ben when I had taken enough Dutch courage to try to pull someone. Belinda smiles at me as I explain how it went. Eventually, she puts me out of my misery and says it is fine. She knew that I did not make it in because of my hangover. She finds it amusing and cannot imagine seeing me hungover. I am relieved that I am not in trouble and that she does not think any less of me. I ask for assurance and she reassures me that it is not an issue and finds it funny that someone like me would get drunk.

ON OUR WALK back to work, I ask Belinda what it feels like to get a hangover as I explain that it feels different for me. She tries to think back to her last time. She finds my question strange; it's as if I am worried that I have caught something. I explain that my tummy still feels weird even though my head is fine. I also mention that I may have had food poisoning from having a kebab. Belinda shows no concern and suggests that it must be my time of the month. I tell her that it is not for another two weeks. Belinda shrugs her shoulders and advises me to go to the doctors if it continues to persist.

I have my answer and will not bother to text Mercedes for her opinion. I will leave it a week to see if the dull pain in my abdomen finally goes away.

I decide to go shopping tonight when I get home from work.

WHEN I GET HOME and park up, I walk over to the supermarket. I always buy the same things and so I do not need to make a list. I also walk along the aisles in the same order every time.

As I walk through the tinned food section, I catch sight of a man at the other end of the aisle. He is slim and taller than me. I wonder if he is single as he is carrying a basket rather than pushing a large shopping trolley. I cannot see a wedding ring and so at least he is not married. As I am making glances at him, he notices me and I quickly turn away, feeling embarrassed.

After a moment, I glance back at him and notice he is attractive. He glances back at me again and smiles which makes me smile back and I feel that there is something there. As I go to grab a tin of soup from the shelf, acting all cool, I grab a bottom can and the entire stack of cans falls off the shelf. I try to continue acting cool as I struggle to stop the cascade of tinned food falling to the ground. I nervously smile at him as I struggle to deal with the embarrassment. He stares down at me with pity as he walks past me.

This is typical for me. The one and only chance of potentially getting to know someone new and I ruin my chances.

A member of staff has heard the commotion and comes over to help me. He advises me to leave it and he will handle it. I try to make light of the situation but he gives me a disappointing glare as he starts to put back the items. He makes me feel small as I step away and continue with my shopping.

I finish paying, but there is one thing that the supermarket did not have. I drop off my shopping and pack away the frozen and chilled food, then go to the nearest convenient shop to buy a specific type of dental floss.

WHEN I GET to the shop, I find my favourite brand and walk up to the counter to pay. The man behind the counter is the owner, an Indian man. He puts the item through the till and points at a handmade sign.

It is a worn-out sign written on notepaper, covered in strips of dark yellow Sellotape, on the back of a piece of black brittle plastic. The sign says that a card payment has to be five pounds or more. I am sure that the banks stopped charging for small card payments.

The Indian man is short with stubble and short hair. He stares at me, pointing at the sign, while I explain that all I have is a card and I do not need anything else. He asks me to buy sweets or crisps to make up the difference. I gawk at him as he suggests I buy a lottery ticket. I tell him that I never buy those things and I have no interest in winning the lottery. I survey the shelves to see what I could buy but am at a loss as there is nothing I want.

The man keeps telling me to buy a lottery ticket as it is cheap and that I never know. I feel I need the dental floss as I am O.C.D with my teeth and scared of the dentist. Eventually, I give up and accept the lottery ticket.

He then asks me to choose numbers. I give him an annoying stare and he takes the hint and mentions that the machine can choose random numbers. I finish the conversation by saying that I will certainly not win the lottery if generated by the same company. The man ignores my comment as he prints off the ticket. I go to throw it on the floor but he urges me not to. I roll my eyes and dramatically place it in my back pocket to make him happy.

AFTER I GET HOME, I sit in my living room wondering about Ben and why he has not texted me or called me yet. I do not know whether to text him first to find out if he is not interested or has a reasonable excuse for not calling.

I cannot believe in the last few days that I have been drunk, pulled a guy and paid for a lottery ticket for the first time. I cannot believe I wasted three pounds on a ticket I will never get back, only to get my dental floss. I will not be going to that shop again.

5

FANCY MEETING YOU HERE

While I am getting ready for work, I think about how long it has been now, with this funny tummy. Thinking back, I have been feeling this dull pain about two weeks now. We are in November and we went out in October. I hoped it related to the kebab and that it would subside.

The pain comes in waves then goes away for a while. It has put me off my dinner slightly as I think that is irritating the pain more. I have stopped grazing and only having three light meals a day. I have avoided heavy food like pasta, red meat and chips and focused more on salad, fish and refined soup.

I had hoped it related to alcohol or food poisoning as it would have taken a week to recover. It is now worrying me how long I have been feeling like this.

I made the bad mistake of looking up my symptoms on the internet. It could be any number of things, such as gallstones, gallbladder inflammation, gas, inflammatory bowel disease, appendicitis, ulcer, gastritis, gastroesophageal reflux disease, pancreatitis, gastroenteritis, parasite infection, endometriosis, kidney stones, abdominal muscle injury, abdominal hernia, lactose intolerance, gluten intolerance, menstrual cramps, peritonitis, serositis, ischaemic bowel disease, vasculitis, abdominal aneurysm, abdominal organ injury from trauma to name but a few. I have no idea what half of these are, but I am worried in case they are life-threatening.

I decide to leave it for another week before going to the doctor. If I have a sudden turn before the end of the week, I will see the doctor sooner. Until then, I will get on with my monotonous life.

In the meantime, I will carry on taking the painkillers when it is too uncomfortable.

· · ·

WHILE DRIVING TO WORK, I keep having thoughts about Ben. I still have not heard from him since that night two weeks ago. I did not have the guts to text him or call, as that is the man's job.

I won't lie, I am upset, as I thought he genuinely liked me and wanted to see me again. Each time I receive a text message, I quickly check to see if it's from Ben. Each time I am disappointed.

Every night, I envision what our conversations would have been like if he phoned or what we would text about. I also dream about our first kiss and wonder how soon we would sleep together. Explaining that I have never been with anyone might make it awkward.

DURING LECTURES, I find myself forgetting where I am with my PowerPoint presentation and skipping a sentence. I compensate by sipping a cup of water to gather my thoughts and retracing my speech.

My students are oblivious to my poor delivery. They seem to be too focused on jotting down my formulas, diagrams and scripture.

I feel like I am lecturing for the first time again as I have butterflies. My mind is in conflict between thoughts of the subject I am teaching and pining for a relationship, wanting to know why Ben has not been in contact.

DURING LUNCH WITH BELINDA, I question why I am the only person on the planet who cannot naturally fall into a relationship. I wonder why I have to keep my eyes open for when it may happen, which has been never. I only half-listen to what Belinda has to tell me about her morning at work and how her weekend went. My thoughts are taking over our normal conversations and I find myself saying 'yes' and 'no' at the appropriate times.

It has been years since I allowed my thoughts to be consumed with wanting to be with someone. It feels like yesterday when I last had these thoughts. I do not like having these feelings and thought I had buried them away forever.

IN THE AFTERNOON, marking assignment work seems to make the remaining hours drag by. I keep losing my place on my students' report pages when checking paragraphs that warrant grading.

I think about what I am going to do tonight when I get home; stare at my four walls, feel sorry for myself for having no regular social life and knowing how my evenings will go. Not hearing from Ben has magnified how unhappy I

am with being single. Ben gave me a glimpse into how great it could be to
have a boyfriend, long-term partner or husband.

Now I realise I really want that. I have always wanted that. I would give up
my career to have that because work does not complete your life. Work is
pointless if you have no one to share it with and tell that person how your day
went. I would even go as far as to say that I would trade my life for that.

WHEN I GET HOME and finish having my dinner, I have a sudden urge to go to
the gym, so I get ready to go out. I have no idea why I want to exercise, as
Monday is not my normal night for the gym. It is after nine o'clock when I
have my gym clothes on. I have my rucksack with spare clothes to change into
and toiletries for a shower afterwards.

I head to my twenty-four-hour gym.

I BEGIN by following my gym app and performing the appropriate stretches.
Once I have fully stretched, I start my workout with a twenty-minute gentle
jog to work myself up. I then go on to free weights and work on my legs bum
and arms, and finish by doing sit-ups and squats.

After my jog, I go to walk off the equipment when I bump into another
gym member. All I see is a grey T-T-shirt and the person's midriff. Without
glancing up at the person's face, I apologise and go to walk off.

I am taken aback when I hear a voice call my name and apologise. It is
Ben! This takes my breath away as I am not expecting to see him in the gym I
go to, of all places. I want to question why he never contacted me, but the
shock makes me tongue-tied and I have no idea what to say.

Ben smiles at me as he wipes the sweat from his brow with the back of his
wrist. 'I come here four times a week and I have never seen you in here. Are
you new?'

I gather myself from the shock and stutter a little, 'I have been going to
this gym for a couple of years now. How long have you been coming?'

Ben appears surprised as I wait for his answer; 'About two years as well. I
am surprised that we have never bumped into each other. Apart from tonight,
what days do you come?'

I have to think; 'Mostly weekends, Friday, Saturday or Sunday. I mostly
run outside all the other days.'

BEN NOTICES sweat on Sarah's forehead and beads of sweat cascading down
her neck by her ear. He finds her attractive because of it and is slightly
aroused by her presence. He hates the thought of not having been able to call
her over the last two weeks.

He finds her even more sexually attractive now. He pauses for a second as he realises how much he has missed her.

THERE IS an awkward silence between us until Ben says something, 'That would explain why I have not seen you around.'

I guess the conversation is over now; 'I'll leave you to it.'

I honestly thought I had a chance with him. I cannot make eye contact and I walk past him with my head down.

Ben goes to speak, but stutters to get out his words, 'I...I'm sorry I did not call you. How I wish I could.'

I turn round to face him and say, 'It's okay. You realised that I am not your type and had a change of heart. It's okay.'

BEN STARES at me and eventually smiles and says, 'No, the opposite. I did not remember that I had a holiday booked. I did not think to let you know. When I came back, I had a death in the family, so I was not in the right frame of mind to go on a date. But you were always in my thoughts. Wondering if I left it too late. Wondering if I would have the chance to call you, then leaving it too long for you to be up for a date. Maybe you would have already met someone.'

I suddenly feel guilty for making it all about me. 'I am sorry to hear that. Please accept my condolences. Were you close to them?'

Ben accepts my sincerity. 'Thank you. It was my uncle. Yes, we were close and it was expected. We knew that he only had up to a year to live. We had that time to be with him and say our goodbyes.'

He makes me even more guilty for feeling sorry for myself because he did not call me. I feel like asking him out for a coffee to console him.

I cannot help but fancy him more after he tells me about his loss. 'If you ever want to go for a coffee and talk about it, you can call me. If you have misplaced my number, I can give you it again.'

Ben smiles; 'It's okay.'

I assume he means that he does not want to ever call me as a friend to talk to, so I say, 'No worries. I guess you have enough friends to talk to. Why wouldn't you? Duh.'

Ben almost laughs; 'I mean, I would like to go out with you. Not only talk about my uncle.'

I suddenly light up and smile, saying, 'That would be nice.'

Ben is keen to make our date sooner rather than later. 'Can we go out for dinner this Saturday?'

I find myself being a little kid as I stand there gazing at him, 'That's a date. What time are you thinking?'

Ben thinks about it for a split second, 'How about five o'clock? We can go for a meal followed by drinks afterwards.'

'That would be great.'

Ben finalises the itinerary, 'I will text you by Thursday to confirm where and also get your address. Was thinking of picking you up.'

I stare at the floor and gush as I cannot believe he would prefer that. 'That sounds great. I will see you then. You can text me anytime.'

I can't quite believe I will be going on my first date ever! 'I look forward to it. Wishing away the days already.'

With that, he walks away and I cannot stop gazing at his back and his bum through his baggy tracksuit bottoms. I find him sexually attractive and noticed how sweaty his T-shirt was. The encounter with him has given me the impetus to finish my exercise routine.

I CONTINUE to feel great inside when I get home and take a shower and dry myself to get into my pyjamas. I find myself struggling to get to sleep as I imagine how our date will go.

I am still awake after two o'clock and feel renewed energy and it is keeping me from falling asleep. I cannot stop thinking about Ben as I lie staring at the ceiling and feeling uncomfortable in my sleeping position.

Now, I struggle to find a position to get to sleep as I toss and turn under the duvet. Every time I glance at my clock, only a few minutes have passed. I wonder why time flies when I am enjoying myself, but when I am bored, time goes so slowly.

It is not until close to four o'clock in the morning that I finally doze off to sleep.

As I AM DRIVING to work, I find the two cups of coffee are helping to keep me awake. I am already wishing for lunchtime to come and I have not even arrived at work yet. I want to tell Belinda about bumping into Ben and that we are going on a date this Saturday.

Thinking about Ben makes the journey to work pass quicker.

WHEN I GET to the car park, I cannot wait till lunchtime to tell Belinda about my date with Ben, so I text her before I leave my car. Sending the text to her makes the date more real.

I was hoping to get a text back by the time I reached my office but nothing. I am disappointed that she did not reciprocate my happiness.

.   .   .

BEFORE MY TEACHING STARTS, I have time to reflect on my life and think about what I want to achieve now. I am ready to focus on my love life now and want to settle down with a husband and have kids. There is nothing more I want to achieve in my career apart from keeping doing what I love. Through the natural course of progression through my career, I will end up being head of my faculty in years to come. I might even change university to accelerate my progression.

However, I am financially content and my affairs are healthy. I do not want for anything material.

So, logically, I am now ready to share my life with someone and prioritise my personal life. It is time to spend the next thirty-two years focusing on finding the right one, getting married and having children.

I THOUGHT I would never hear myself admit that I wanted a relationship and to start a family. I thought I would never be ready, finding the next excuse to avoid the topic. My parents will be pleased to hear that I am starting to date.

I do not know if Ben has triggered my priority or it has crept up on me unexpectedly. It did really affect me when he did not contact me. I think that if it had happened a few years ago, it would not have bothered me and I would have accepted it and moved on.

WHILE I HAVE BEEN ESTABLISHING my new-found outlook on life, the dull pain in my stomach has interrupted my thoughts.

It is annoying me now as I had assumed that the pain would ease off over the past couple of weeks. I have not yet made an appointment to get checked out. I plan on seeing my GP during the fourth week if this persists. The pain is not so unbearable that I cannot manage it. I have been taking painkillers as and when my pain threshold is reached. I know it cannot be my appendix as I have been told in the past that the pain is excruciating. Also, the pain is across my belly and not on one side where my appendix is.

I decide to look again on the internet since I have a spare five minutes before the next lecture.

While I search, the list of results includes symptoms of stomach cancer. I click on the link to bring up the symptoms. These include loss of appetite, sometimes accompanied by sudden weight loss, constant bloating, feeling full after eating a small amount, bloody stools, jaundice, excessive fatigue and stomach pain which may be worse after meals.

I am not experiencing any of these apart from stomach pain, so, for the moment, I rule it out.

.   .   .

DURING LUNCH WITH BELINDA, I ask her if she received my text this morning as I did not receive a reply. She tells me that she did but could not reply as she was between meetings. After she explains, she is keen to know everything about Ben and when our date will be.

I remind her of how we met and how we bumped into each other at the gym by chance. She listens to me intently. I make sure I do not leave anything out as I go over every detail. I have her full attention.

After twenty minutes of telling her the whole story, with some interruptions by her affirming that she heard correctly, she is really happy to hear that I have finally focused on my personal life to find happiness. I tell that her that I am not thinking he is the one but I will try to find someone that will make me happy, regardless of who that is. The more I think about meeting someone, the more I am ready to move on to the next stage of my life. Belinda is very encouraging about putting my social life first now as I am established in my work role.

THE REST of the afternoon goes fairly quickly and it does not feel that long before it is time to go home.

As I walk to my car, I hear my mobile make a noise to let me know that I have received a new text. I am taken aback when I see it is from Ben. I naturally think it is the worst, that he is cancelling the date on Saturday. As I nervously read the message, I realise the message is asking if it is okay to call later tonight. The message puts a smile on my face and I quickly text back. I suggest calling after seven as I know I will be finished with my normal routine by then.

Once I send the text, I start to drive home. I do not check for a response, so I have something to enjoy reading when I get home.

6

IT'S A DATE THEN

It is now after seven and Ben should be calling any minute now. I rushed my food down so I could have an uninterrupted chat with him. I have a glass of red wine to make me relaxed while I wait for the mobile to ring.

CLOSER TO QUARTER PAST SEVEN, my mobile eventually rings and I get excited about seeing his name on my phone. I leave it to ring at least four times before picking up.

I feel more nervous now as I pause before acknowledging him, controlling my eagerness to speak, 'Hello?'

BEN IS confident on the phone, 'It's Ben. The guy you bumped into at a night club and again at a gym.'

I play along with him; 'Are you the one with the bad dance moves? And also, barely does any exercise?'

Ben laughs down the phone, 'And your dance moves are any better? By the way, I thought you looked sexy in your gym outfit, hot and sweaty.'

I cringe at the thought of my sweaty body appearing sexy. 'You're kidding. I thought I looked awful with no makeup and perspiring so badly.'

Ben laughs again at my response. 'Trust me, you were looking good that night.'

I change the conversation to steer away from me. 'So, what have you been up to in the last twenty-four hours?'

Ben still finds me funny; 'A lot. I had a shower when I came home. Then I slept for a few hours. Went to work for half-past eight. Stayed till five and then came home. Had dinner and now I am on the phone to you. How about you?'

I am unable to make my day sound any better, so I say, 'Pretty much the same. Do you have any idea what you want to do this Saturday?'

Ben has stopped laughing and I hear silence for a brief moment, 'I was thinking of dinner. Go early for dinner, and afterwards, head to a bar for a few drinks.'

I like the idea of that, so I tell him, 'That sounds nice.'

I WONDER what else to talk about as I struggle to think of something. There is an awkward silence, then out of the blue, Ben finds a new topic of conversation.

'I went to Denbigh Secondary School which was nearer my home. What school did you go to?'

Ben does not pause before telling me, 'I went to Oakgrove school, in Middleton. What college did you go to? Assuming you did.'

He makes me smile as he tries not to offend me, 'I went to MK college.'

Ben shows an interest in what I studied; 'What subjects did you study?'

While I collect my thoughts, I find his voice soothing, 'I studied science. How about you?'

Ben sounds like he is hesitating; 'Erm, I studied Law. At the same college.'

I perk up; 'What year did you study there? We may have been there at the same time.'

Ben sounds surprised as well and I hear excitement in his voice; 'I was there between two 2002 and 2004. What about you?'

I think back to when I was in college and work out how old he could be. 'I was there between 2003 and 2005. You must be thirty-three.'

BEN GUESSES MY AGE; 'And you must be a year younger. Thirty-two. So, what do you do for work?'

We both find it amusing that we could have bumped into each other at college. 'I am a lecturer. And you?'

Ben states the obvious, 'I am a solicitor.'

I know that solicitors deal with variations of law and want to know what he is practising. 'Do you deal in criminal, family or corporate law?'

Ben sounds impressed with my questioning. 'I practice family law but specialise specifically in fertility and family estates.'

My mind is blown away, 'Fertility? How did you get into that?'

. . .

BEN APPEARS to find me a breath of fresh air; 'I have never had a woman ask me these questions before. Normally, they only ask about what my hobbies are and what I like.'

He makes me feel good about myself. 'I like to know more than simply hobbies or likes and dislikes. How did you get into specialising in fertility?'

BEN CONTINUES, 'One day, a client came into the office and was offering to donate her eggs to a friend, so, she wanted legal advice on how to go about it. The practicality, morals and ethics of going ahead with it was her dilemma. I looked into it and I was referred to after giving her advice.'

He makes me like him even more. 'So, what was the outcome?'

Ben comes across as awkward on the phone, 'She was able to donate her eggs to her friend with no problem. What do you lecture in?'

'I LECTURE IN ASTROPHYSICS, so I talk about planetary stars, black holes and potential life forms.'

We end up talking for almost three hours, not realising that is almost half-past ten. We both agree to end the conversation. After we finalise Saturday night, we finally hang up.

It finally sinks in that I will certainly be going on my first date.

AS I GET ready for bed, I imagine the next five days will drag for me as I am excited for Saturday to come along. While I finish changing into my pyjamas, I picture in my head how I think the date will go. I imagine him opening the doors for me and offering to pay for my meal and drinks. However, I prefer to pay my own way.

My stomach is now getting butterflies with the thought of having dinner with Ben and finding out more about him.

DURING THE REST of the week, the hours and days appear to drag past. I desperately want Saturday to come round quickly. My one-hour lectures, which would normally feel like twenty minutes, now feel like two hours. Doing my preparation for my lectures and marking papers seem to take longer to complete. The drive to work and home also drags on now.

I hope the date does not flash before my eyes after waiting for so long for the week to end. I wished that we had talked in the middle of the week, then it would have only been a couple of days to wait rather than five days. At the same time, I would not have been able to wait till later in the week to speak to him.

Luckily, we have been texting each other which has helped to ease the frustration. The messages have been generic banter rather than getting to know each other properly. At least we will have a lot to talk about When we finally reach date night.

The night before is worse as I know it is less than twenty-four hours until the date. The last time we texted each other was Thursday evening, agreeing to wait for Saturday to come.

NOW IT IS FRIDAY, I feel even more nervous. It feels like time is slipping past now when it seemed to drag at the start of the week. I feel I do not have enough hours now to get ready for tomorrow.

To calm my nerves, I go shopping for an outfit after work. I drive to Oxford shopping centre as it is close to work and I do not want to waste time trying to get to the shops in Milton Keynes.

I want to wear something casual and so I choose not to venture into buying a dress. I search for a smart pair of fairly dark blue jeans and a nice off- white blouse. I will also buy a new pair of dark brown high heels. I know exactly where I can get what I want so only have to visit three shops.

During my shopping, I think about how the date will go, again imagining us kissing at the end of the evening. I wonder where he will take me for a drink after dinner, wondering if he would fancy having a dance or merely drink to silliness like how we first met.

I wonder how dinner will go. Will we be tongue-tied, struggling with what to say to each other, or will I waffle on about nothing and bore him to tears? I have told myself to start the conversation with how his week has gone and what he has been up to in the day time before our date. I will also read up on online social stories in case I have nothing else to talk about.

By the time I finish buying my outfit for the evening, I eventually get home a little after seven o'clock. After I get home, I take my clothes out of their packaging and lay them on my bed. Then I take my shoes out of the box and place them under the pair of jeans. I admire my choice of clothing and see myself wearing them.

Afterwards, I heat up a can of soup for my dinner. I open a bottle of white wine to drink with it. As I sip my beef soup, I think about how my tummy feels.

ALL THIS DISTRACTION has taken my mind away from my dull stomach pain that has still been coming and going. Getting excited over a potential new relationship has been a good way to take my mind off my health worries.

I still plan to make an appointment on Monday as it will be three weeks since the pain first came about. I still have not had any bleeding, but it has been affecting what food I eat and how often.

I hope the restaurant offers a nice light dish that will be a main meal. I hope he does not want to have a three-course meal, as I will only be able to stomach a main course and possibly one drink.

Great, I am now worrying about whether the date will go well with my eating habits; worried that he will think I am a weirdo dictating how many courses we will eat. I try to not let it bother me and focus back on the excitement of going on the date.

7

IF I FORGET TO SAY, I HAD A WONDERFUL TIME

As I stir from my broken sleep, I cannot believe Saturday has finally arrived. I could not stop thinking about my date as I tossed and turned in bed last night. Now I only have to wait over six hours.

While I am still lying in bed, I collect my thoughts on how my stomach is feeling now. It feels slightly sore still and so I will undoubtedly go to see my GP next week. I will drive to my surgery first thing in the morning to make an appointment. I hope that this does not ruin my date with Ben.

I think I will lie here for a bit and see if I doze off back to sleep to catch up. Then I will go for a gentle run, stomach permitting. After that, I am hoping it will be time to get ready. I quickly send a text to Ben to let him know that I cannot wait for later.

It is a surprise to get a text back straight away, echoing the same thought. It reassures me that he is still keen to go out tonight. I keep reading his text as it makes me smile and I almost laugh to myself.

My eyelids start to feel heavy and I drift back to sleep.

ONCE I WAKE UP AGAIN, I see it is close to eleven o'clock, so I get out of bed and into my running gear. I will have a shower after I get back.

As I go to put on my trainers in the hallway, I catch sight of something out of the corner of my eye. It makes me glance twice. All of a sudden, it is gone now and I was unable to register what it was. I think nothing of it and drive to Willen Lake to go for a run.

There are two car parks at Willen Lake. One is a less popular choice as it feels far away from the main lake and quiet. I use the busiest car park to start and finish my run.

. . .

WHEN I GO for my run, I don't bother with carrying a music player. I prefer the peaceful quietness that I find while running around the lake. I run along the grass of the path to cushion my legs as my feet impact on the ground.

As I get halfway round, I start hearing music and it sounds really close. I turn my head round while still keeping my pace. I assume it is coming from one of the houses that are scattered around parts of the lake. There is nothing obvious and so I assume that the music will dissipate as I move away from the sound.

Funnily enough, the song I can hear in my ears is 'Keep on Running' by Spencer Davis. I feel someone is taking the mick out of me. The sound is still at the same pitch when I first heard it. I am startled that someone could be following me. I also realise that the lyric 'Keep on Running' keeps on replaying like it is stuck. I run faster to outrun the sound but it is still close by. I start to get petrified and sprint.

I have roughly ten minutes left of my run and feel that I have the stamina to sprint the last ten minutes. I simply want to get away from the music but I cannot get away from the repetitive lyric. It is starting to worry me now as it does not feel humorous anymore.

I look around to see if there are any other people who could be running, walking their dog or driving nearby, but no one else is around.

Towards the end of the run, the music suddenly goes away as quickly as it started. I cannot believe I heard the song so clearly, yet there was no one around.

As I drive back home, I do not think any more of it.

I JUMP in the shower to quickly make myself human again and wash away the sweat and body odour. It is after one o'clock and so there are only four hours left to go before Ben picks me up and we go for something to eat. He has kept the choice of restaurant a surprise. All I know is that it is in Woburn and we are getting a taxi so both of us can drink. He is going to leave his car at my place and pick it up the next day. I have offered to make him breakfast if he manages to come over before eleven.

I have a simple lunch of butter on toast with slices of cheese. I swallow my lunch with a cold glass of diluted juice. Bread is okay for my stomach.

WHILE I EAT my cheese on toast, I think back to my experience around the lake. That music was so clear and felt like I was standing next to the audio player.

. . .

WITH ONLY AN HOUR and a half left to go before he comes to pick me up, I change into my new clothes and put on light makeup. I feel myself getting excited as I put on my new clothes; after all, this is my first date!

I spent years enjoying characters in romantic films, hoping that my dates and relationships would go like theirs. The female characters always seemed to be like me, especially the personality of the woman in the 'Bridget Jones' series. I have been known to watch the same film over and over again to lose myself in the story plot.

To pass the time away, I check to see what is on television, flicking through the channels, trying to find something that will make the remaining time fly past.

FINALLY, I hear my buzzer go on my comms and pick up the handset to check it is him. I press the buzzer to let him in through the door downstairs. I tell him that I still have a couple of things to do, so he should come up. I want him to see my flat before we go out for the evening.

WHEN HE ARRIVES, I show him around, a tour which takes all of thirty-seconds. I notice he has come a bit early and so ask if he fancies having a quick drink here before we walk across to the restaurant. He likes the idea and asks what I have in the way of alcohol. I open my fridge to see if I have any wine. Why didn't I check before offering it? Luckily, there is half a bottle of rosé left in the fridge and I ask if that is okay. He says it is fine and I grab two wine glasses from the cupboard.

As I pour the wine, I make conversation; 'You found my place okay, then?'

Ben appears caught off guard as he inspects the kitchen; 'It was straight-forward, actually. Thought finding which building was your flat would be a nightmare. Imagined having to call you to find it.'

He makes me laugh as I finish pouring two glasses. 'Normally my friends are having to call me. So, you did really well.'

Ben keeps the conversation flowing. 'What did you get up to today?'

I try to sound interesting; 'I went for a run. Around Willen Lake. I like going there because most of the time it is nice and quiet. How about you?'

Ben finishes taking a sip of his wine and adds, 'I played football this morning and then basically came home and started getting ready for tonight. So, it went quite quick for me.'

The wine is hitting me straight away and I feel my shyness subsiding. 'So, are you taking me to MacDonald's or a slightly more expensive restaurant?'

Ben finds me amusing, 'No, Burger King. I hope you don't mind. It was the only place available tonight.'

I laugh again, finding his sense of humour more attractive, 'I am allergic to beef. Is that going to be a problem?'

Ben smiles at me, almost laughing; 'They do salad. Is that good enough?'

We both laugh at each other and I feel that this evening is going be a blast. It is finally time to walk over to the restaurant which is only a few minutes' walk away.

As we leave my apartment, I go to close my door when something catches my eye in the hallway. I do a double-take when I see a squirrel standing upright, waving me goodbye from the other end of the hallway. I laugh to myself as if it is too silly to believe. I nervously wave back at the squirrel, thinking to myself that I should stay off the wine.

Ben notices and asks if I am okay. I tell him that there was a fly bothering me and laugh nervously at him as I lock the door. Did I actually see a squirrel waving to me?

As we leave my building and walk across to the restaurant, I blurt out to him, 'Before we get too drunk, I really want to tell you one thing. If I forget to say, I had a wonderful time.'

Ben glances at me as we continue to walk and smiles at me as his way of saying thanks.

ONCE WE REACH THE RESTAURANT, which is called Browns, we are taken to our table and the waiter asks for our drinks order first, before letting us peruse the menu. We agree to get a bottle of wine between us. I let him decide which wine to order.

Ben breaks the silence by asking me a question. 'What do you still want to achieve?'

I find the question ambiguous. 'What do you mean?'

Ben makes himself clearer; 'What do you still want to achieve in life?'

I think about what I have always wanted to do, 'There are a lot of things that I want to do. I want to travel, but not travel as in trek the Himalayas. I mean travel like seeing parts of America, the Grand Canyon, New York City, Golden Gate Bridge and...'

Ben is puzzled why I have gone quiet. 'What? You can tell me. I promise I won't laugh.'

I feel like an idiot for even thinking it; 'I want to go into space. It is now achievable. I don't mean space as in an astronaut, but going into a plane and flying over the surface of Earth. I would love to be able to do this in my life-time. In twenty years, it could only cost you like a thousand pounds instead of a hundred grand.'

Ben does not stare at me like I have two heads, 'That would be cool. I would sell my house on my death bed to go spend my last day flying into space. So, apart from going into space, what is stopping you from travelling America now? Each year you could go and explore a new place.'

I never thought about it like that, so I replied, 'I looked at it as in taking a couple of months off and doing it all in one go.'

Ben is about to say something when the waiter comes back and asks for our order. We did not give ourselves enough time to choose. We both randomly choose our dishes on the spur of the moment. I choose to have a salmon dish with a side dressing and Ben chooses steak with mashed potato. After the waiter takes our order and walks away with a smile, we continue our conversation.

Ben has a curious stare. 'So, will you look to take two week's holidays per year to start seeing parts of America?'

I had never thought of taking holidays abroad. 'Now you have me thinking, I think I will have to start planning my next holiday.'

Ben smiles at me as if he gave me great advice. 'It would be great if we both went. I have never been to America myself. I have mainly visited different parts of Europe.'

I am curious to know where he has travelled; 'Okay, so where have you been in Europe?'

Ben tops up the two glasses, then says, 'Been to Paris in France, Spain, Portugal, Brussels, Amsterdam, Warsaw in Poland and also Sharm El-Sheikh. I almost left that one out.'

I feel jealous as he tells me this, 'Wow! I am envious of you. The furthest I have travelled was London. Shopping. I wish I had made the time to travel.'

Ben appears surprised to hear that, 'Well, it is not too late. Look at taking a holiday next month. Something simple, like going to Paris.'

The thought of going by myself scares me, so I said, 'I would need to go with someone. I am not that brave. Did you go with friends or a girlfriend to those places?'

From his facial expression, it looks like Ben feels sorry for me. 'I went with a mixture of friends, old girlfriends and even by myself. A wedding one time, in Portugal. An old Uni friend.'

Our dinner arrives and distracts us from our conversation. We both compliment each other on our choices of food and tuck in.

As I go to cut into my slim slice of salmon, I notice something in the corner of my eye again, behind Ben. I panic a bit, hoping that I am not visualising a squirrel again. Unfortunately, it is not a squirrel but five of them.

The five squirrels are wearing waistcoats with the Union flag on the front and carrying walking canes. They also have a straw hat in their hands. They walk upright on two legs in a single file from behind a couple's table behind Ben. They are rustling their straw hats as they come out in full view. I glance at the diners next to the squirrels, expecting them to see what I can see, but everyone is engrossed in their own conversations. I am the only one who can see them.

THE SQUIRRELS PUT their straw hats on to their heads and their ears poke through the rim. They start dancing in sync like they are performing a musical on 'Britain's Got Talent'. I can suddenly hear the music that they are dancing to. I recognise the music to be 'Then He Kissed Me' by The Crystals. As I gaze at them, I realise what I am doing and quickly focus back at Ben with a nervous smile and giggle, trying to laugh off the situation.

Ben looks round and glances at me oddly, wondering what I am watching. I quickly tell him that I was gazing at a pair of nice shoes a woman is wearing. He stares at me with a puzzled expression and asks why I was laughing at her shoes if I liked them.

I wave my hands as if a fly is bothering me and stutter the word 'nothing'.

THE SQUIRRELS SMILE as their eyes see through me. I turn my head behind me, to see if they are staring at someone else behind me. I brush my hair back to be discreet, so Ben does not become suspicious again.

I STUDY my glass of wine, wondering if my drink has been spiked. The song is still playing loud like there is a band playing in the restaurant. Then, out of nowhere, the squirrels' performance suddenly ends abruptly and they walk backwards, in single file, to where they came from behind the couple's table. The last squirrel disappears and then reappears to bow, with his straw hat in his hand, before disappearing one last time.

BEN HAS BEEN busy eating his food and is almost finished. I find myself eating hurriedly to catch up with him. I also take a gulp of my wine as if to wash away what I have seen. It felt too real to be a hallucination, even though no one else noticed or could see and hear what I could.

The music dissipated at the same time as the squirrels walked away.

I quickly snap out of my weirdness by asking Ben a little more about himself. 'So, what country would you like to go to next?'

Ben goes to answer my question as I double-check that the squirrels will not be coming back. 'I would like to look at going to America. Is there something behind me?'

He catches me staring again, so I snap out of it while I give him another nervous smile. 'So, so, do you know which part you would like to visit? That is America, right?'

Ben sighs as I use his forehead to focus on. 'I would like to go to Los Angeles and go to an American football game. As well as see Hollywood. I have to say, you look gorgeous tonight.'

I have never had anyone say that to me before. 'I don't know what to say to that. I am not used to compliments. You look nice tonight as well. This is the best date I have ever been on. I mean, this is the first date ever.'

Ben smiles at my comment and our eyes lock over the empty plates. It takes the waiter to distract us as he asks us how our meal was. We both tell him it was great and he leaves us with a dessert menu. My tummy feels full and I suggest that we could share a dessert if he wants one. He likes that idea and I let him decide. In the end, he chooses a cheesecake.

When we finish our shared dessert and the bottle of wine, Ben pays for the whole meal. I insisted that I pay my half and put my card on the receipt but he will not hear of it.

AFTERWARDS, Ben takes me to a wine bar in Woburn, not far from Milton Keynes, which means getting a taxi. We go to the taxi rank around the corner from the restaurant. We get one almost straight away and head there.

ARRIVING AT THE BAR, we find a table and order drinks for the rest of the evening. The night goes by quickly as we talk about nothing. We make each other laugh and luckily, I do not see any more squirrels or hear any music, other than the tunes played in the wine bar.

We both slowly get drunk together as we mix our drinks between cocktails and spirits. We drink till past midnight then both decide to head home. We share a taxi again, stopping at my flat first.

When we arrive, I go to automatically get out of the car as if we are mates. He taps me on the shoulder to get my attention. I turn to him after I clamber out and we bump our noses as we try to kiss. We both gaze into each other's eyes and make a second attempt.

The taxi driver turns round in his seat and stares at the two lovebirds in the back. Ben pulls away first, apologising to the taxi driver for keeping him from his job. We both agree to see each other tomorrow at eleven o'clock.

I watch the taxi drive away until I can no longer see the car. I then hobble to my flat, enjoying how the evening went.

8

THE DAY AFTER

As I get ready for bed, I check the time on my bedside clock and think to myself that it will be only ten hours to wait till I see him again.

After I change into my pyjamas, I clean my face of makeup and brush my teeth as I think about the date. It puts a smile on my face as I brush my teeth. I now know what a date feels like and it was perfect. I hope there are many more to come.

I WAKE up with no hangover this time, but with a dry mouth and the taste of Coke, vodka and possibly gin. I guess no hangover is put down to not drinking Jaeger Bombs. I feel half asleep though, but a shower will cure that.

While lying in bed, I check the time and it is gone eight o'clock - that gives me two hours to shower, put on a little makeup and go to the supermarket across the road if need be. I did not check my fridge or freezer to see if I needed to buy anything extra.

ONCE I HAVE BEEN in the shower and feel more human, I check to see what I do have in my fridge and make a list of what is missing. I want to cook Ben sausages, eggs and bacon and have some crusty rolls to serve with it. I also want to make fresh ground coffee using the cafetière that I have not used in months, so, I have to give it a quick clean.

When I check the fridge, I realise I need sausages, eggs, bacon *and* crusty rolls. I have none of the main ingredients. All I have is half a bag of potatoes, one carrot, half a cucumber, a half carton of orange juice and a tiny bit of ground coffee. Wow, I need to buy everything!

I send a quick text to Ben to make sure he is still coming for eleven o'clock and leave putting the makeup on until he texts back that he will be over at the agreed time.

I wish I had the courage to ask him to bring spare clothes and stay over. It would have been nice to wake up with him and spend our time buying groceries and chilling out on my sofa. But that can be an excuse to go on another date.

WHILE I AM in the supermarket, certain aisles remind me of my episode the other week when I thought someone had taken a shine to me until I knocked over the cans of soup, then the time when that idiot shop owner made me buy a useless lottery ticket to make up a five-pound spend. I wish I had won the lottery. In saying that, I never did bother checking the numbers. How funny would it be if I did win some money? A fiver would be good enough for me to cover the cost of my dental floss and the ticket!

I spot the same member of staff who helped me with clearing the sea of cans from the floor. He remembers me as he smiles at me and I smile back, embarrassed. I quickly grab a tin of baked beans as I walk past him.

ONCE I AM BACK HOME, I get out a frying pan and a saucepan and start unpacking the food. I switch on the kettle for the coffee and prepare to start cooking.

Cooking makes the remaining hour fly by as I put the cooked sausages, bacon and eggs in the oven to keep warm. I wonder why I did not shower after cooking all the food so I do not smell of smoke. Oh well, it is too late now. I will put on some perfume to mask the smell of sausages.

As I finish buttering the crusty rolls, my intercom buzzes. Ben is only five minutes late. Good timing.

I TAKE Ben's coat and hang it up on the hook I have behind the front door. I walk through the hallway to the living room where I have my dining table. I have already laid out the plates and condiments, basically, ketchup and brown sauce, which I also bought from the shops this morning.

BEN APPEARS IMPRESSED as I think he was only expecting a bacon roll and a hot drink. While he sits down, I take the two plates and rush into the kitchen to transfer the cooked food from the oven to the plates.

As I am dishing the food up, Ben walks in and observes what I am doing. He rubs a hand against the bottom of my back affectionately. He is taken aback by how much effort I have made and kisses me on the cheek as a way of thanks. It turns from being a kiss on the cheek to a full kiss on the lips. I notice we both still have the fresh taste of mint from brushing our teeth. I welcome the passionate kiss as it lingers for a few moments. I turn to face him to make it more comfortable to kiss him properly. After a few minutes, we remember the food is going cold and he grabs my plate as we take our food into the living room.

WE TALK about how well last night went and straight away we are talking about a second date and, this time, not leaving it till the weekend. He suggests going out on Tuesday this week. I am happy to go along with that and I suggest we eat in this time. Ben offers to cook at his place as I have cooked for us this morning. He says that he will make his favourite dish which is spaghetti bolognese with a particular spicy sauce to go with it. I cannot wait to taste his cooking.

After we finish eating, I assume he wants to go home right away but I am hoping he will stay at least till mid-afternoon. We end up sitting on the sofa to allow the food to settle and one thing leads to another and we start romantically getting closer. Neither of us is in a hurry to end what I guess is our second date. We do not encourage second base as we enjoy each other's company; I am simply lying on top of him and making pecks on his lips.

Eventually, we decide to put on a DVD, which I have underneath the television in an old wooden T.V. stand I took from my parents' house. My taste in films is a bit embarrassing as I watch him choose the best out of the bunch. He mocks my taste, but in a teasing way. He makes me laugh as he comments on our choice of films to watch. Eventually, he chooses a nineties' comedy film.

I end up resting my head on his shoulder with my legs folded up on the sofa as he holds my hand.

IT IS GONE five o'clock when the film finishes and he helps me to clean up the plates and utensils. He texts me his address for Tuesday and we arrange to meet at seven o'clock.

I kiss him at my door before he eventually leaves.

IT IS ALREADY DARK when Ben leaves. The flat seems lonely now I am by myself again. I wish our relationship was at the stage of moving in together. It would have been nice to have him keeping me company before going to bed.

I have nothing to do to make the evening pass before going to bed. I start to reminisce on what we were doing earlier and what conversation we had, including last night. The blackness outside of the window makes me feel like I am the only person on the planet. I find November and early December depressing as it is the lull before the festivities and time off work.

I close the curtains in the living room and bedroom and keep the light on in the hallway as well as the living room. I do not like my apartment to feel completely dark. To fill the void, I check what clothes I have to wear for during the week and pack away any that I don't need.

By seven o'clock, I have finished my chores and wonder what else I can do for the next three hours or so before bedtime. I give Ben a text to see if he got home safely. I tell him again that I had a wonderful weekend with him and cannot wait to taste his cooking. He texts back saying he is worried now in case I do not like his spaghetti in a joking way. We end up chatting for a full three hours before we both notice it is time for bed. I thank him for giving me company as I was bored and void of distractions. He reciprocates, saying that he felt depressed coming home to an empty two-bedroom house, wishing that he had stayed for longer. Neither of us wanted the day to end, and if we had known, he could have stayed later,

At least we both share the same feelings and are on the same page.

9

AM I GOING MAD?

December is around the corner. The next day, at lunchtime in the 'The Lamb and Flag', I am keen to tell Belinda how my date went. I tell her before she has a chance to ask. I talk at her at a million miles an hour so as not to forget any of the details and to prevent her from interrupting. Belinda comes across as overwhelmed by my theatrical story-telling. She is not sure where to start after I finish telling her how the dinner went, drinks afterwards and the next day. I do not mention my hallucination of the squirrels as it is way too embarrassing.

Belinda finally says something; 'So, I guess you are going to see each other again.'

I smile to myself, 'We are going to chat on the phone tonight and we are next seeing each other on Wednesday.'

Belinda is happy for me and tells me how glad she is that I have finally met someone.

OUR FOOD ARRIVES at our table and as I am about to tuck into my fish and chips, I see a whole fish, un-battered, on my plate. It lifts its head sideways and starts singing at me. I do a double-take while trying not to show Belinda that I am having another hallucination. The fish is staring at me with sadness in its eye. It is singing in a man's depressed voice, 'Let the River Run' by Carly Simon. It makes me jump and I try to not draw attention to myself in front of Belinda.

I peer down at the solemn singing fish and it makes me nervous as I fidget with my hand behind my neck. Belinda wonders why I am not starting on my meal. I nervously smile at her as I decide to start on the chips around the singing fish.

Belinda shows a concerned expression. 'Are you okay? You seem to be skirting round your plate.'

I nervously laugh as the fish continues to sing with a weepy expression, 'Nothing. I am just thinking about Ben. Laughing about the date.'

Belinda peers over my plate and asks, 'Are you sure you are okay? You are staring at your fish oddly.'

I flick my hair to hide my nervousness, 'I am fine. So how was your weekend? Get up too much?'

Belinda dismisses my oddity and tells me about her weekend, 'The usual. Seeing family. We had my parents come over so they could see their grandchildren. Not as exciting as your weekend. You going to eat your fish?'

I use Belinda to distract myself from the singing and the moving of the lips. Eventually, it stops and my battered fish returns. I give a sigh of relief and quickly tuck into my fish so she does not think any more of it.

I need to book myself an appointment with my GP as I am now getting worried. If it is not my stomach problems, it is my new-found oversized imagination. I am not sure if this happens to coincide with doing new things such as getting drunk and finding a first boyfriend. I think my mind and my body are struggling with new drastic changes in my life. I must be having a nervous breakdown. Yes, that must be it. My heart is ready for Ben but my head is struggling with it.

Belinda snaps me out of my thoughts and we talk about work during the remainder of our lunch. I will certainly make an appointment when I get back to my office.

As I PICK up the landline, I wonder how long I have had my tummy upset. I count on my fingers and compare it to how long I have been dating Ben. It has been four weeks that I have been living with the pain. I have only been taking painkillers occasionally - I have not been living on them.

I feel my stomach to see if the dull pain has gone away. At the moment, it feels totally fine and so I feel an idiot for making an appointment. I should have made an appointment within the first two weeks of it starting. But Ben has been a distraction and the weeks have flown by.

I have only had hallucinations for a week and they are inconsistent, so I am not worried about them and will not be mentioning it when I call at my local surgery.

My HAND STARTS to shake as I pick up the handset as this makes it real that I have a problem. I take a deep breath before dialling my local surgery. When the receptionist picks up, I go to book the next available space after five o'clock. As I confirm which time, she asks me what it is for. The question makes me nervous as I do not want to say that I am hallucinating. I pause to think if I want to be honest with symptoms.

The woman on the phone asks if I am still there and I quickly respond so she does not hang up. I eventually tell her that it is my stomach as I am too embarrassed to tell her about the hallucinations.

I was going to make the appointment if the stomach pains did not go away, so, Sod's Law, I will be totally fine and my hallucinations will get worse and drive me insane.

The next available appointment is this Friday at quarter to six. Now that I have made the appointment, I feel a relief as I am finally doing something about my stomach pains. I am putting my hallucinations down to so many changes in my life.

During my last class session for the day, I start hallucinating again.

While my students are reading their textbooks and answering questions, I continue marking the essays handed in. While I am going through my students' work, I hear a tapping on the window. I glance over at my students to see if they have responded to it. I see they still have their heads down while I can still hear tapping on the window. I glance over at the window being tapped and I can see a gnome smiling at me. As I nervously laugh to myself, I observe my students again, expecting them to react by now. But they are not hearing the tapping noise.

I am now glad that I made that appointment with the doctor. If it was not for my abdominal pain, I would not have made the appointment. Now, I will be honest and tell the doctor about these visions.

My nervous laughter turns to me feeling slightly scared. It is a typical pottery gnome with a live painted clay face. It starts to dance along the window ledge from one end to the other, on the outside. It waves at me with a big grin. I continue marking the papers, pretending that I cannot see it. The gnome tries to get my attention in a thick Bristolian male voice. I check my students again, but they cannot hear the talking pottery gnome. I try not to react otherwise I could get their attention.

The next second, it appears on top of the desk right next to me. It makes me shriek. I startle my students as they raise their heads at me and I giggle, embarrassed. I tell them that I thought I saw a mouse. After I scare them, my students continue their work. I cannot believe I jumped like that.

The gnome is still there and I have the urge to reach out with my forefinger to try to touch it. As I poke at the gnome, I notice one or two of my students observing me. I freeze and then casually go back to marking. I glance up to see if they are still watching me. Some of them are occasionally raising their heads up discreetly while still working.

I can still see the gnome on the desk making conversation with me. He tells me that I deserve to be in a relationship and that he thinks I am very attractive. He jumps up and kisses me on the cheek. I do not feel the kiss but feel his presence next to me.

I manage to get through the lesson without drawing further attention to myself. None of the students acknowledge the elephant in the room. I thought they may laugh at me but they simply walk out making indistinct chatter among themselves.

WHEN THE ROOM IS EMPTY, the gnome has gone and I start to tear up. I am worried now as I have had an episode in front of my students. I really hope that it is not the stress of meeting someone new in my life.

I am also worried if Ben finds out and stops wanting to see me. I wonder if I will have the same illness as the American John Nash who suffered paranoid schizophrenia, achieving a Nobel prize. This is starting to worry me.

DURING MY DRIVE HOME, I do not encounter any more hallucinations, but it worries me that it may occur. I keep my wits about me in case I have another episode. I focus on the road as a distraction. I keep checking in the rear-view mirror in case the police are behind me and think my driving is erratic. I can imagine the police thinking I need a straitjacket.

The journey feels longer as a result of being paranoid.

WHEN I GET through the door, I feel relieved and if I have a hallucination now, it will be fine. I turn my thoughts to Ben as a way of distracting me from my health worries. I cannot wait until I talk to him at seven.

I will not let him know about my two problems as I do not want to lose him, not when I have only just met him. I think I am getting a little worried that it is something bad; a sign that there is worse to come.

I am bored waiting for the time to come round, so I switch on the television and watch the news. I sip on my chicken soup as I hear that someone is still to claim their lottery winnings, I think I remember this being mentioned last week and wonder why they are bothering to mention it still. If no one has claimed it now, what is the likelihood of someone suddenly phoning now? Besides, it is only three million pounds. It is not like it is a hundred-million-pound lottery win.

THROUGH BOREDOM, I change the channel to find something interesting. While I flick through the channels, I wish I had won the lottery. I could take myself away from here for a while, not permanently but for a bit of respite.

The dull pain is coming in waves again so I take a painkiller to ease the discomfort.

BEN CALLS a little after seven and he starts the conversation; 'How was your day?'

Apart from the hallucination, I tell him how my day went. 'I had my usual lunch with Belinda. Told her about you. She wants to meet you.'

Ben sounds intrigued. 'So, did you tell her how our date went?'

I have to think back to what I told her; 'I explained what we did but not in great detail. I felt sorry for her because she could not get a word in edgeways. I only wanted to tell her the bare essentials, before she interrupted. I felt sorry for her.'

Ben quietly laughs down the phone. 'I feel sorry for her. I am surprised you didn't bore her to death. You didn't put her off me, then?'

I end up laughing on the phone. 'Shut up. She loved my story-telling. You're giving me a complex.'

Ben sounds like he is enjoying himself. 'I hope you told her how perfect I am and how lucky you are to be with me. Don't laugh, I am being serious. I am perfect. Stop laughing.'

I have to allow my laughing to calm down. 'I thought I would try my best to make you sound good. It may have back-fired and I think she thinks you are a weirdo.'

Ben scoffs at me, 'You always were bad at telling a great story.'

I tell him how much he should appreciate me; 'You're lucky to be with me. I have a perfect body, extremely attractive. And you have completely fallen for me.'

Ben laughs again as I tell him how great I am. 'I was too drunk to notice your looks and great body. I will have to go on a second date to see that. Oh, I forgot, it is this Wednesday. I may have to poison your food now.'

I sigh, 'Yes. We do have Wednesday. I am hoping the next two days will go quick and the evening will go really slow.'

Ben sounds taken aback, 'I want to text you all day, but I do not want the phone calls to be boring and for us not to have anything to talk about on Wednesday. A catch twenty-two.'

It feels nice to share the same thoughts; 'I think the same. I often want to text you in the day time but I am not sure if you are too busy to be interrupted.'

Ben also says the same; 'I do not want your phone to beep in the middle of your lecture. I have no idea how many lectures you give per day.'

The way we are thinking makes me feel that we are in a relationship already. 'We can discuss this on Wednesday.'

Ben likes that; 'I would like to do that.'

We continue our conversation talking about our family backgrounds again for a recap and talk about any embarrassing moments.

Ben shocks me by telling me about a time when he went to a work event when he was a student at college. He would not tell me who the company was but that it was a supermarket. It involved a comedian and a few entertaining women. He tells me that he went there sober because he was warned what would be happening on the night. He mentions that the women performed sexual acts as entertainment involving a double-ended rubber dildo and other props. The bit that made me burst into fits of laughter was when he ended up being taken on stage, in front of all his work colleagues, to be pleasured by two women. The bit that made me laugh uncontrollably was when he could not sleep on his front as it was so sore. He explained that the women were too rough with him as they both jointly pleasured him. I cannot stop laughing loudly as I picture how it would have happened.

'I cannot believe that happened to you. I don't know which is worse, you being pleasured by two strippers or the fact that you were sober.'

I can sense Ben feels embarrassed for telling me and maybe thinks I am offended, 'I cannot believe I told you. I am embarrassed now.'

I make it clear that I am not judging him; 'I think it is funny. And that is your past. Besides, I have already fallen for you.'

BEN GOES quiet on the other end causing me to ask if he is still there. Phew! He is and he admits he has also fallen for me. We talk for another few more minutes before finally hanging up.

We ended up talking for almost two hours but it felt like half an hour. I did not want to hang up even though we both had things to do before going to bed.

SURPRISINGLY, the next two days go by quickly. Before I know it, it is two o'clock in the afternoon on Wednesday. I have quite a lot of essays to mark which will take me the rest of the afternoon.

What has helped is that we both agreed to text each other during the day which has made my days more enjoyable. It has allowed me to do a U-turn and has finally allowed me to tell him about my upset stomach. It is going to make me more relaxed in his presence now he knows about my issue. I will be more relaxed now that he knows that I may behave weirdly if my tummy plays up.

However, I have still not told him of my strange sightings of singing squirrels and fish. I do not want him to think I am a nutter.

. . .

As SOON AS I get home, I get ready for tonight. I have a quick bath to make myself feel human again. When I am finished in the bathroom, I go to get changed. I put on a pair of dark blue slim cut jeans with a thin cream jumper. I wear my hair in a ponytail. I put on pumps with my outfit and wait around for half an hour before leaving to go round to his house.

I end up checking social media on my mobile until it is time to go.

10

CAN'T BELIEVE THIS FEELING

This is my first time in Stoney Stratford, the area where Ben lives. He told me that he lives in a two-bedroom terrace house in a fairly new estate that is off a small roundabout on Hayes Road.

When I arrive, I find that parking on the road is a bit of a challenge. Each house has its own space allocated and barely any visitors' spaces. It takes some time to find an unofficial space big enough for my car.

Once I park up, I realise the estate has poor street lighting and so, it takes time to find his door number. I have to call his mobile to get help finding his door number. Ben opens his front door to see if he can spot me.

AFTER A COUPLE OF MINUTES, I finally reach his house.

HE GIVES me a welcome smile and we hug each other before going inside. I can smell his cooking and the aroma is delightful. His home feels cosy and warm as I walk through the short hallway that leads to his living room at the back. His small kitchen is midway between the front door and the living room. He has a table in the living room already laid out with knives and forks, including placemats for the plates. He offers me a cold soft drink as he knows I am driving back home. He is sweet when he asks how my tummy is and tells me not to worry if I cannot eat all my food.

I walk with him to the kitchen to keep him company while he finishes waiting for the pasta and Bolognese sauce. We both discuss our day at work; his was slow and he says he could not wait until tonight. That makes me feel very special and the feeling is mutual!

I watch him overseeing the two saucepans gently bubbling when suddenly, Ben walks over to me and we kiss. We end up turning pecks on the lips into a full passionate kiss as I am standing against the wall. I can feel something by my hip which makes me wonder what it is. I assume he has a lighter in his pocket even though he does not smoke. I go to move his lighter as it feels uncomfortable. He jerks his body away from me as I try to move it from digging into me. After a few seconds, he presses up against me again and I feel his lighter digging into me again. I try to be discreet and I jump when I realise what it is. After I have felt it, he gazes into my eyes with a smile and accuses me of having an effect on him. I blush as I cannot believe I have given him a hard-on. This is all new to me.

The food almost overcooks as our smooching makes us lose track of time.

DURING DINNER, we laugh about some more of our past adventures. I tell him about the time I went to my friend Sarah's wedding. I fell up the stairs of the reception and my skirt went over my head. I was wearing underwear covered in giraffe print!

Ben tells me that he wished he was there so he could admire my bum in a tight pair of knickers. He makes me blush again as we stare into each other's eyes.

I glance at the clock on the wall and wish the time would go slower. My original plan was to stay until ten and be in bed by half-past. I only have forty minutes left in his company.

After we finish dinner, we move over to the sofa where we start to get more intimate. I feel him getting aroused again as he presses his body against mine. Even though this is my first ever encounter with a man, I find it natural to move his hand under my jumper. I find myself motioning him to stimulate my nipples. They get hard straight away by him simply brushing his palm over my breast. I start to breath deeper as I experience unknown pleasure that I used to envy when I heard my friends telling me about their relationships.

I immediately feel myself getting wet which, at first, made me think I had peed myself. The sensation causes me to grab Ben hand from rubbing my breasts to putting his hand inside my jeans. Ben does not need telling twice as he puts his hands inside my soaked underwear. I feel him put a finger inside my labia which makes me shudder from the sensitivity. I part my legs so I can give him more room to pleasure me.

I DO NOT WANT to go home tonight and will be happy for him to pleasure me all night. Ben starts to nibble on my ear lobe and at first, I am not sure why he is trying to bite my ear. It is not long before I realise that this entices my arousal causing me to feel an explosion inside my vagina. This is what an orgasm must feel like. I think to myself that his hand must be drowned in my already soaked pants. I now want to play with his cock and find out for the first time what it is like to grab one in my hand. Ben makes it easier for me to get hold of it and I grab it in the palm of my hand. His cock feels solid like a wooden truncheon. I have no idea what to do with it apart from holding it and gently squeezing it.

Ben doesn't even know that I have not bloomed yet because it has not come up in conversation. Right now, I am not concerned as the moment is taking over and I do not want this experience to finish abruptly. I feel what I assume is an orgasm coming on as my body starts to stiffen and I find myself guiding Ben's fingers to stimulate a certain spot. I feel like I am about to break his hand as I really want to keep the rhythm going, as I reach a thunderous spasm like electricity going through my body.

BEFORE I KNOW IT, I reach ecstasy and, out of nowhere, I give out a groaning sound that shocks me. My body jerks several times as waves of multiple energy flows through my body and I feel a patch of my underwear completely soaked through. I hope he does not think I am a rampant nymphomaniac from the reaction I gave when he brought me to orgasm.

I also notice that my hair is slightly sweaty and a bead of sweat trickles down from my forehead along my cheek.

Throughout all this, poor Ben's manhood has been squeezed to death. Once I recover, I suddenly remember the stories I was told by my girlfriends. So, I start to jerk him off by sliding my sweaty hands along his shaft. I use his quirky vocal sounds as guidance to whether I am doing it right as his breathing gets deeper. Eventually, I feel fluid dribbling on my forearm and his cock becoming soft. I cannot believe that, a second ago, I performed my first ever masturbation on a man and actually made him cum. I end up awkwardly wiping his cum on his tummy as the slime spreads thinly on his skin.

I can smell a faint scent of our pheromones mixed together. We both end up briefly falling asleep while we let our heightened emotions subside.

Ben wakes me up and whispers in my ear that it is gone ten o'clock and that I should be going if I want to be in bed by half-past ten. I do not want to go and wish it was Friday night so I did not have work to go to. It takes me a while to wake up and get myself off the sofa.

As I go to get up, the thought of Ben seeing a visible wet patch around the crotch area of my jeans worries me. I quickly peer down to see if it is obvious as it felt like water was splashed on me. Luckily, it has not soaked through. I will need a shower before going to bed, though.

We passionately kiss outside the door before leaving. We both acknowledge how much we both enjoyed dinner and afterwards. Eventually, I leave and we arrange to speak to each other tomorrow.

. . .

OVER THE NEXT couple of days, we text each other more frequently about what we are doing and how much we have enjoyed each other's company. By Thursday evening, we agree to date exclusively and we become boyfriend and girlfriend.

It feels surreal saying to myself that I have a boyfriend. I never imagined that I would find someone on my night out with the girls. I merely assumed I would get drunk and then go home.

The last five weeks have been a blur. If someone said I would be in a relationship in the next five weeks, I would have thought they were crazy. I now have a glimmer of hope that I will marry and have children like the rest of my friends. Before, I assumed I would never be given a chance of finding anyone.

A COUPLE OF DAYS LATER, I tell Belinda at lunch about my date. I miss out the intimacy part and tell her about how the meal went and how much I am falling for him. She does try to pry into whether we did more than have a meal, but I simply play it down. I tell her that we are taking it really slow and we are only staying at first base. Belinda finds our relationship boring and makes out that she would have slept with him by now, or at least hit second base. She makes me smile when she says that and I reminisce over my first foreplay.

I SEEM to enjoy work more, now that I have a proper social life away from lecturing. I have a fresh pair of eyes and feel a skip in my beat. I think my students have picked up on it as my lecture theatres are fuller than usual.

I project my presentation with more enthusiasm and dramatisation as I talk about the next part of the syllabus. The next slide I put up is a galaxy outside of our solar system. I describe it in more detail than I would normally do. I even cause some of the students to quietly laugh to themselves.

WE HAVE ALREADY DECIDED to see each other from Friday and spend the whole weekend together. He also offered for me to sleep over on Sunday night if I decide that I want to stay. I cannot believe that the next time I see him, he will be my boyfriend.

I DO NOT WANT this part of my life to end or be ruined by my current issues. I pray to God for the first time, begging him not let this moment slip through my fingers.

. . .

FRIDAY COMES ALONG and I am at C M K Medical Centre. I came straight from work. Ben still does not know everything about my condition. I stare at the television screen waiting for my name to come up with the room number and doctor.

Being in the doctor's surgery is making my problem more real. My palms are feeling clammy as I nervously wait to unload my problems. I am the last person waiting in reception.

I feel like I am outside the headmaster's office, waiting for a verdict. Luckily, I am not seeing things.

Eventually, my name appears on the screen along with Room 25.

I KNOCK on the door and walk straight in. My doctor for today is a lady of similar age to me. She asks me to sit down and tell her what the problem is.

11

DOCTOR, DOCTOR

It is the beginning of December. Taking a seat opposite, I confirm that my problem is stomach pain. She asks me to show her where the pain is, so I indicate the spot on the right side.

She feels around my stomach, pressing firmly to see if I hurt anywhere else. I do not feel any other discomfort. When she presses on the sensitive area, I wince not realising how much more it hurts. She automatically tells me that she is confident it is my appendix. She says that she will give me antibiotics. She tells me that if it was serious, I would have a fever or I would not be able to walk or stand. While she moves back to her computer, she asks how long it has been painful. I tell her that it began around the end of October, so about four weeks. The doctor quickly reassures me that it is nothing to worry about. So, I take the prescription she writes out and go to the pharmacy. I have to take the course for two weeks, which means I can still have a drink over the Christmas period.

I still choose not to tell the doctor about my visions as it is too soon to worry about it now. I will wait another couple of weeks and mentally monitor how frequently I have an episode.

If I had an episode in front of her, I would see it as a sign to tell her, but it did not happen.

She tells me that if the pain persist and gets unbearable, then go straight to hospital.

Now it is December, I have been on a few dates with Ben. It is going from strength to strength and we are never bored with each other's company. We have still not slept together yet but we spoke about it and we both agreed that we will do it when we fall in love. So, in the meantime, we kiss and cuddle and have long foreplay sessions. We are content with having other ways of intimacy.

Our dates have included ice skating, visiting a nearby National Trust property and enjoying romantic meals in.

As we have only been properly dating for four weeks, Ben and I are not going to be sharing Christmas Day together. We are not ready to meet each other's parents for now. We will be staying in touch via texts and phone calls when we get the chance.

In the meantime, Ben and I are going to see each other tonight. I will tell Ben tonight that I saw the doctor today and tell him what the outcome was.

I cannot believe we have been seeing each other for almost five weeks. It seems longer as we feel we have known each other for years.

We now end up having foreplay at the end of every date at either his place or mine. We tend to end the date early to allow for intimacy. He brings me to climax each time. I manage to bring him off most times as well.

I finally tell him about what has been causing my upset tummy. He is glad I told him and relieved that it was not as serious as cancer. He tells me that he was concerned at one stage but did not want to worry me. I find it sweet that he is so considerate.

It is now Saturday, the last weekend before Christmas Day. On our current date, Ben suggests we go to the zoo not far from Milton Keynes. They have a nice trail you can walk along which has rows of trees on either side. Some parts of the trail have the trees overhanging, appearing like an archway. There are still some autumn leaves lying along the trail.

The cold weather is crisp and we can see our breath when we talk or breathe out. We are both dressed very warmly so we can enjoy our walk without being uncomfortably cold. I have put on a slim white jumper over a vest and a pair of jeans. My brown coat is nice and thick and I finished the outfit with a pair of walking shoes.

Ben is wearing a blue shawl neck jumper and also a pair of jeans and hiking shoes. His coat is thin, but wind and waterproof

We had lunch in a pizza restaurant, then waited till later in the afternoon to go for a walk, so there would be fewer dog walkers and other couples and we can walk along, holding hands, as if we are alone.

While we walk, we talk about having our own Christmas Day on Christmas Eve. We decide to open our presents for each other with wine and mince pies. I tease him by promising that I will wear my Christmas underwear to get his heart racing. Ben likes the idea of that, naturally, and asks me to promise him.

I tease him some more by telling him that I will give him a lap dance as part of his Christmas present. He knows by now that I have no earthly idea how to be sexy when performing a lap dance, hence why he laughs at the idea and ridicules me with the prospect of me flailing around.

One section of the trail has such dense forest that you can get lost in it. Now, I would not ordinarily suggest this, but I offer to give him a blow job hidden among the dense trees. We are like two school kids on a field trip and we go off and hide. When we feel safe that no one will see us if they walk past us along the trail, I slowly unzip his jeans.

Because of the suspense, I feel him getting slightly hard. When I take it out, it is semi-hard and the cold is not doing his cock any justice. I gently put his manhood in my mouth and slowly bob my head.

BEN IS ADMIRING Sarah working her mouth up and down his cock and how her head bobs up and down. He likes the feel of her hot breath on his cock. It feels weird for him as he can feel the cold air on his shaft as she pulls off his cock. He can feel her saliva on his skin going cold and hot as she swallows and pulls away.

He ends up putting his hand behind the back of her woolly hat and motioning her to go deeper inside her mouth. Now and again, Sarah glances up at Ben and their eyes meet as she works her mouth on his shaft. Occasionally, she swirls the tip of her tongue around the end of his cock and rubs it under her nose. Ben pushes her head away and waves his cock so it gently slaps against her cheek and she fights to put it back in her mouth. Ben finds her sexy as he watches her struggling to regain her hold. He finds her sexy as he teases her, pulling out of her mouth.

THERE IS something promiscuous as Ben teases while I try to finish giving him a blow job. I love the feel of his cock in my mouth. It feels weird to hear myself say this as, six weeks ago, I had no experience and never thought I would ever enjoy giving oral.

Whether it is too cold on his manhood or he has never had oral sex performed in a public area, I do not manage to make him cum. However, I can see from the expression on his face that he enjoyed it. I give one more quick lick of his gorgeous cock before putting it back inside his warm jeans. He quietly thanks me for pleasuring him.

. . .

WE BOTH DECIDE TO head to for the local pub for a hot drink and to get out of the cold.

THE PUB IS popular for dog walkers and other couples and we have to squeeze through a crowd of locals to get to the bar. We order a glass each of mulled wine. When we go for second and third drinks, I stick with mulled wine and he moves to drinking Coke after his first drink.

We find a seat by the fireplace which makes us feel cosy. We end up talking more about our families and what his uncle, who recently passed away, had meant to him.

He was close to him and so it hit him hard. He contracted a brain tumour and suffered for a year taking chemotherapy. He aged overnight and his quality of life spiralled downwards. If I had that, I would rather avoid the treatment and try to achieve as much as I could of the things I had always wanted to do.

He tells me that he came round a lot to his parents' house. His uncle would take him fishing and introduced him to golf. It was his uncle who took him out and gave him a lease on life. His parents left him to his own devices when growing up. His stories make me envious of his childhood and make me wish I had experienced something like that.

I AM intrigued what it would be like to have cancer and have questions like, 'What does it feel like to live with cancer?' 'Do you feel you are being punished for something you did in your life?' 'Do you regret smoking if that caused your cancer?' 'Do you hate the person who encouraged you to smoke, being naive?' and so many more. I feel so at ease with Ben that I can pose these questions to him.

I PAUSE to find the right way of asking these questions, 'Ben. I want to ask you a question and it is merely curiosity. If you feel uncomfortable telling me, I will not be offended.'

Ben sips his Coke before giving me his answer, 'Um, what kind of question? My favourite sex position or my favourite sport?'

He is amused by his own comment which makes me smile, 'I have always been curious to know what it is like to have cancer. Is it okay to ask you something about it?'

Ben surprises me as he is totally fine with it, 'Sure. It won't be anything that will offend me.'

With his permission, I am keen to let out all my niggly thoughts, 'Did your uncle ever talk about his thoughts while dealing with cancer?'

Ben's mind takes a step back and I can see he is thinking it through. 'He never openly told me exactly what he was going through, but I could see it in his eyes. His facial expression and his eyes told me it all. He had regrets. He thought he was being punished for being an awful husband and father. He tried to work out what part of his life had caused this punishment.'

I am fascinated by his answer but I have more questions. 'Did he suddenly start believing that there was something out there, like a god?'

Ben's expression lights up like it is a debate. 'Oh yeah! Towards the end, the very end.' Ben is starting to get emotional. 'Excuse me. I'm okay. When he knew this was it and there was nowhere else to go, he began wondering what was going to be on the other side. Not having any idea what would be in the afterlife was frightening for him. I remember when I was by his bedside at home and he wanted to tell me about what his thoughts were. He told me that he would be more scared if it was simply pitch black because the thought of never seeing another person scared him. He wanted to see his dad again, to tell him things he regretted not telling him.'

It is nice hearing about reality and not tip-toeing around the taboo subject. 'Did he feel that he caused the cancer to come on? Wish he had eaten certain things or made certain healthier life choices?'

Ben is really patient with me; 'He ate reasonably healthily. He never had those thoughts. He had no other regrets other than being a bad husband and parent. He never smoked or did anything that everyone knows is bad for you.'

'Do you have any other questions?'

There is something else that popped into my head; 'Did he feel embarrassed having cancer in case people assumed it was smoking-related or because of a bad diet?'

Ben finds my questions quite thought-provoking. 'That is a good question. I can't answer that. But I assume he wasn't because he wanted everyone that was important to him to know that he was going, give them time to say their goodbyes and vice versa. Any other questions?'

There are no other questions that spring to mind, 'No. But I really appreciate your patience with me. It has always been a subject that I have wanted to ask about. I would never wish that on anyone, even if they were the worst person in the world.'

Ben agrees with me; 'It is a very aggressive killer. The moment when the nurse said that it would be best if he was at home as he would be more comfortable around his family, we knew it was a polite way of saying that there was nothing else they could do for him. Knowing that it was a waiting game was the hardest part. Even if you know when the D-Day will be, it does not prepare you for the inevitable. You don't get closure.'

As he tells me, I come close to tears as I visualise being there with him back then. I think he has managed to compartmentalise his bereavement and rawness, considering it only happened four weeks ago.

I check that he is okay; 'Are you coping alright? You're not merely putting on a brave face?'

Ben takes a sip of his drink before answering, 'I had a year of preparing for it. His life was away from home, so I do not have anything in my face to remind me. It hurts that he is no longer here but I am more relieved that he is no longing hurting. He is free of pain. I know my cousin is the opposite to me. He was her dad and she has a lot of unresolved matters that she did not make time to address.'

I naturally grab his hand as I gaze into his eyes to show that I am here for him. I am not only here to be entertained or find fun; I am also here for the bad times. I am not going anywhere. Ben can see that and we gravitate towards each other as we go in for a kiss.

We change to another subject, to a more upbeat conversation on celebrities who have done stupid things. We go back to laughing.

WHEN WE GET BACK HOME to my place, we are immediately in the mood for intimacy. We go into my bedroom and I suggest he lies on my bed. I go to pull his beige jeans down with his help so I can get access to his cock.

I cause him to get an instant erection using my small hands and start gently smacking his cock against my cheek. It has the desired effect of making sure he is fully hard. I poke my tongue out and lick the end of his manhood and watch him at the same time.

Ben raises himself on to his elbows so he can see what I am doing. We lock eyes as I continue to lick the end and try to be seductive. I feel like I am still a complete amateur as I am making it up as I go along, but our connection makes me feel comfortable and not embarrassed.

I gradually start to stroke his shaft while still continuing to lick the end until, eventually, I take it in my mouth. My hair falls over my face and he gently pushes it away so he can see me giving him a blow job. Now and again, I take it out of my mouth and rub it across my chin and smell his cock to take in his scent. He is circumcised which makes it easier for me, even though I have never given a man a blow before. I can only imagine having the hassle of keeping the foreskin back.

I can feel his body starting to stiffen and assume he is close to climaxing. This encourages me to build up my rhythm to keep him stimulated. It is not long before, without any warning, he shoots his load. His cum goes up my nose and some almost goes in my eye. I feel his semen dribbling down my cheek. I am curious to know what semen may taste like compared to how it smells and so I lick some of the semen still oozing out.

I can only describe the feel of it going down my throat like what I imagine raw egg white would feel like. The taste is weird, yet it does not necessarily have a particular flavour. It tastes how it smells. It sounds stupid to say, but I feel closer to him now I have tasted his cum.

I watch Ben shudder as he gets over his orgasm and find him pulling away as I lick the end. I guess it must be very sensitive for him. When he has recovered, he wants to give me oral.

This will be the first time for me as I am used to him using his hands to pleasure me.

I STAND up and pull my blue jeans down in front of him and take them off completely. I stand there in my cream knit jumper and white cotton G string.

We swap places and I let him remove my underwear. He smells them before putting them aside. I make a sarcastic disapproving noise as I squint my eyes at him.

I naturally part my legs, slightly raising my knees up at an angle. I watch him slowly crawl towards my crotch as we keep eye contact. I see his tongue coming out as he gets closer to my labia. As he strokes me with his tongue, I find it quite rough, which surprises me as I assume it would feel smooth.

As he gets within the folds of my vagina, his rough tongue does not seem so bad anymore and I feel myself lubricating quicker than when he uses his hands. I find myself parting my legs further to allow him to get inside deeper. I can feel his chin nudging my bum cheek and that stimulates me. It feels weird as I am not into anyone getting near my bum hole.

He now starts to suck at the top of my vaginal entrance and I try to move his head to go deep when I feel an instant arousal. I have no idea what he is doing to get me so excited. I feel he has a piece of flesh between his lips that feels bulbous. The feeling takes over my body and I start to freeze before having an almighty orgasm and I groan deeply as I have multiple spasms. Ben is still sucking on it as I try to move his mouth away from my now over-sensitive vagina. At the same time, I do not want this wave of emotion to end.

When he finally lets go, I see my juice dribbling down his chin and I find myself apologising to him. I have never cum that hard before or spilt that much love juice out of my labia. I have to ask him what he actually did then.

He tries not to laugh at his accomplishment as he crawls up to lie next to me. He brushes against my breast which makes me jump as they are ultra-sensitive now. We end up kissing passionately even though we only gave each other oral sex. I thought I would taste myself on his tongue as we French kiss, but thankfully I cannot tell. It would feel weird for me to taste my own cum.

He squeezes my bum as we press our bodies closer together. I cannot believe that I have experienced oral sex.

12

HOLIDAYS ARE COMING

It is Christmas Eve night, just after seven o'clock. I finished work today for the Christmas holidays. I do not go back until the second week of January. The students finished for the holidays in the second week of December, however, my work doesn't finish there. I have prep work to do for the next semester.

Ben is coming over tonight at about eight o'clock and we are going to stay in and have mulled wine with mince pies. Ben is making the wine from scratch with a recipe from the internet. He is going to sleep over and have Christmas breakfast before we go to our own families.

Knowing that we will be having our usual intimacy, I shower and put on fresh clothes and wear my favourite perfume.

I finish getting ready early, so I have time to catch up with myself.

BEN ARRIVES PROMPTLY at eight o'clock and I buzz him in. When Ben comes in through my door, I cannot help pouncing on him and kissing him passionately. I am grateful for him coming into my life. He obviously finds my action unexpected but welcomes it.

After kissing him, I hug him like my life depends on him.

We then go into my pokey kitchen and I watch him prepare the mulled wine. He is so focused on getting the simple recipe right. Once the concoction is on the boil, I unpack the mince the pies I bought from my local supermarket across the road. Luckily, I had no episode in there.

I suddenly think of the present I bought him. I have not put it under the miniature Christmas tree I have on the window sill. I quickly get it from my bedside top drawer while he lets the mulled wine simmer away.

.   .   .

ONCE THE MULLED wine is ready, he pours both of us a mug and we drink them in the living room. I organised for us to sit on the floor around the coffee table. I use cushions from my sofa to rest our elbows on or our heads. I have already placed mince pies on a plate on the coffee table. I have coasters on the table for the hot drinks.

We enjoy eating our mince pies and sipping our mulled wine to wash it down. We still cannot stop staring at each other as if we have just met for the first time.

I am glad that my course of antibiotics is finished, as I would not have been able to drink. It feels like the pills have worked, as I do not have the dull pain anymore.

After a few more sips, Ben makes a pass at me and I welcome his advances as I fall back on the cushions for support. He gets on top of me and kneels over me so as not to crush my body. I start pecking him on the lips, enticing him to start kissing me passionately. It does not take long for him to take the hint.

He gropes one of my boobs under my top and that feels good. My nipple is starting to get hard from the squeezing of my breast. It feels so good not to be alone at Christmas for the first time.

EVENTUALLY, we decide to exchange presents. I had not noticed him bringing in mine; I only saw a bag filled with the ingredients. I wonder if he does not realise he has forgotten to bring my present.

I grab his present and wonder when he is going to tell me that he has not brought mine. As I take my time giving him his, I start to feel awkward for him. I nervously smile as I pass it over.

Ben smiles as he receives his gift and I feel embarrassed for him. As I am about to give up hope that he has brought mine, he reaches behind him under my sofa. He laughs at me as he passes over my present.

We both open our presents at the same time and I try to unwrap mine at the same pace as him. When I reveal what he has bought me, I feel that I love him. Wow! I cannot believe I thought that.

He bought me a beautiful pair of dangling earrings set with diamonds. I wait with anticipation for his reaction. After a few seconds, Ben finally smiles and shows his appreciation and kisses me briefly. He likes the watch I bought him! I was not sure how much to spend and asked my girlfriends for their advice. So, I spent close to two hundred pounds to make the gesture feel special.

He puts it on straight away to show me how it wears on his wrist. By ten o'clock, we are ready to go to bed and spend couple time before going to sleep.

. . .

THE NEXT MORNING, we wake up facing each other and wish each other
'Merry Christmas'. I have imagined what this would be like for years. I did
not think that I would still be with Ben when this moment arrived. During
the first four weeks, I kept telling myself that he would dump me any time
soon. Once it got to two months, I gradually started to believe that it would
not end.

If someone told me last Christmas that I would be in a relationship and
waking up to him on Christmas Day, I would have simply laughed in their
face.

Ben has a discerning face. 'What is happening with your stomach pains?'

I tilt my head into my hand and recap what happened in the appointment, 'I went for an appointment...'

Ben is the first to hear this, 'You never told me that you were going to the
doctor.'

I feel awkward for him finding out this way, 'I didn't think it was a big
deal.

Ben comes across as disappointed in me. 'I don't care if you think it is no
big deal. It means something to me. Yeah? Carry on.'

I feel like I have been told off, 'Well, she told me that my appendix is
inflamed and gave me antibiotics to take.'

Ben relaxes, 'So, that will sort it out?'

I reassure him, 'It is only inflamed. If the doctor thought it was more serious, then she would have suggested they should take it out.'

Ben is reassured now and I suggest starting breakfast to move away from
the subject. I sit up, looking around for my pyjamas as I have no clothes on. I
feel totally fine standing up in front of him naked as I find my pyjama bottom
and top.

WHILE I PREPARE an omelette with chopped tomatoes and mushrooms, Ben
comes in and makes some coffee. We talk about how we think our family
Christmas will go. I tell him about what my parents' tradition is and he does
the same.

I tell him that we open our presents in the evening after late afternoon
dinner. He tells me that his family open presents after lunchtime. As we talk
about our family quirks, we start to wish that the other person could come
over for Christmas dinner and present opening.

Neither of us wants the morning to end.

By the time the coffee is ready, our omelettes are ready to eat. We talk
about random things while eating our breakfast. Our topics go from television soaps to political issues in the current media. We voice our opinions
rather than have a debate and laugh about how we voice our opinions with a
dry sense of humour.

I feel like we are a married couple now as we engage so freely with one another. We do not feel that either of us will be judged.

After we have breakfast, we both suggest having a shower together for the first time.

WHILE WE ARE SHOWERING TOGETHER, I naturally gravitate towards his penis as I stroke it under the shower. He enjoys squeezing my bum and reaching underneath to my vagina which feels amazing. I move his hand to my front and part my legs to allow him comfortable access to my private part. He slides two fingers in and starts turning me on. I pour shower gel on his penis and create a lather to jerk him off. Neither of us cums but we enjoy pleasuring each other while washing ourselves.

After we shower and change, we chill out on my sofa and watch Christmas shows on television. Ben does not have to leave straight away as it is only just after eleven o'clock.

We cuddle up together, only half paying attention to the programme.

WHEN IT IS time for Ben to go, we passionately kiss each other goodbye at the front door. I am missing him already before I even close the door behind him.

My parents are expecting me by one o'clock. I put my parents' presents in a used shopping bag and check that I have not missed anything.

WHEN I GET TO MY PARENTS' home, Mum answers the door and walks back into the kitchen. She tells me that they have already started cooking Christmas dinner and I ask if we are eating earlier. She tells me that she is still getting dinner ready for six o'clock.

I follow her into the kitchen to see what she is up to. I can see that the turkey is already in the oven. I am a bit surprised, assuming that we would be eating earlier instead of at the traditional time.

I wonder how long it takes to cook a turkey if she had already put it in the oven before I arrived at half-past twelve.

Mum tells me that Dad is in the living room watching television and that I should go in and see him, leaving her to potter in the kitchen.

WHEN I GO into the living room to see him, he is sat in his high armchair with a can of lager in his hand, wearing a paper hat from a Christmas cracker. He has on a Christmas jumper with the bottom half red and the top half showing a picture of Santa Claus riding with his reindeers against a white background.

He is watching a Christmas edition of a game show. He welcomes me as I sit on the sofa with him on my right.

There is a comfortable silence as we both watch the television. Eventually, my dad asks me what I have been up to. I hesitate at first to mention my boyfriend, so I say 'nothing much' and that work is the same. I ask what my dad and mum have been up to and he says that they have been ticking over. Nothing much to mention on their side.

My dad asks me if I have been on any dates, assuming I am single because I have not mentioned any boyfriend.

I tell my dad casually, in a low calm voice, that I have a boyfriend. It takes him a few minutes to register what I have just told him. He promptly sits up and asks me to repeat what I said. I tell him again, in a casual calm voice, that I have a boyfriend now.

Dad smiles as he turns to face me, 'That is good news. How long have you been together?'

I continue to stare at the television and say, 'Almost a month and a half? Since the start of the second week of November. His name is Ben.'

I think back to when I last spoke to them or saw them and cannot believe I have not seen them in over a month.

Dad asks, 'Did you tell your mum?'

I smile to myself as it feels even more real now. 'I almost failed to mention it.'

My dad is happy for me. 'I thought you were gay. Not that I would love you any less.'

He makes me almost laugh. 'I thought I was a lesbian at one time.'

Dad tries not to laugh which causes me to giggle. I could not imagine being in love with a woman. The thought of even giving oral or receiving oral from a woman is weird to think about. At the same time, I have nothing against lesbians considering my friend Georgina is gay.

I CANNOT STOP THINKING about Ben while waiting for dinner. It is now after four o'clock, three Christmas shows, soaps and game shows later. The Queen's speech was as riveting as usual but my parents love to listen to it.

I have been thinking of Ben the entire time and wonder what he is doing at this precise moment. He told me that his family are all at his parents' house. So, I imagine his household being much busier than mine and his family completely distracting him from his thoughts of me.

I want to text him but feel I will intrude on the time he is having catching up with cousins he has not seen for months. I also do not want the feeling of being ignored by not getting a reply. As I think about wanting to text him, I get a message on my phone. I open my phone to see who it is from, wishing it to be Ben. It is! My heart races as I rush to open his message to see what he has written.

His message is sweet, asking if I wish the same as him, that we were together now. He also asks if it is okay to see me tonight at his place or mine. I am in shock as we agreed to next see each other on Boxing Day night. It means that he misses me as much as I miss him. I do not waste time texting him back to say yes. I want to go round to his house so it does not hurt so much having to leave him rather than the other way round. We agree that I will go over to his house for ten o'clock. That gives me time to go home first and pack clothes for a sleepover.

I feel like my life is complete and I am the luckiest woman on the planet. Nothing can ruin this.

DURING DINNER, my parents ask me more questions about Ben such as his age, his surname and what he looks like. I tell my mum what I told my dad earlier as well as answering my mum's other questions. After I give them the answers, they ask if I am in love. I have to think as I have not even considered it. I have no idea how I will know I am in love. All I know is that I want to be with him more often as time goes by. I cannot stop thinking of him and I enjoy our intimacy and love it when he is inside me. But I do not think that is a sign of love. I would call it infatuation.

My brain is still catching up with how things have been going in my life.

AFTER DINNER, my parents and I swap presents and take turns opening them while playing Christmas songs in the background. It is a tradition to buy five presents per person in our family of three. We stick to a budget of sixty pounds per person. After we open all our presents, we try to find out who bought our presents.

Dad goes out into the kitchen to get Mum and me a drink. My mum likes to drink sherry while Dad gets me a glass of coffee liqueur. I would normally go for red wine but when my dad said he had liqueur, I jumped at the chance.

While Dad is still in the kitchen, my mum asks me more questions about Ben, such as where he lives, what he does for a living, where his parents live and what he is doing for Christmas. I tell my mum that he is a lawyer and works in London. I also tell her that he lives in Stoney Stratford and his parents live in Emerson Valley.

MUM CAN SEE in my eyes how happy I am with Ben and the subject of kids comes up. She is very keen to have grandchildren. She hints that she wants a boy and a girl. I smile at the idea as we both think about babies. Mum asks me how my close friends and their kids are. So, I bring up Natalie, Georgina, Kerry and Mercedes. I tell her the sad news that Mercedes is struggling with conceiving and that she now has to go down the In Vitro Fertilisation route. I also tell Mum that they are struggling to find the money as the hospital is not funding the treatment. Mum feels sad for her and her thoughts are with them. I tell my mum that if I could do anything, I would. I mention how Mercedes loves being an aunt and treats them like they are her own.

Dad finally comes back into the living room to bring our drinks and then goes back to get himself another can of lager.

Mum asks me if I am worried about time passing by and wanting to get married and have kids. I tell her that I think about it all the time and have never stopped thinking about since leaving school, wondering if I would be one of the lucky ones to have the opportunity. I used to be jealous of people at school, college and university who were in a relationship, whether good or bad. I would moan to myself that couples in bad relationships were taking for granted their fortune of being boyfriend and girlfriend. I used to be depressed that I was not in a relationship and would give anything to have someone love me.

I have never spoken to my mum this candidly before and, for the first time, I let her have an insight into my thoughts. Mum feels that she should have known this. I tell Mum that it is not her job to know everything about their child, but that it is only now that I am able to talk about my dreams.

Dad suddenly comes back and feels that he has walked into a mother and daughter bonding. He jokes about leaving the room and to let him know when it is safe to come back. Mum and I glance at each other and smile as Dad sits down and watches what is on the television.

When I feel it is time to go home before I go round to Ben's house, I thank my parents for dinner and the presents. They tell me that I am more than welcome to stay over and sleep in my old bed, but I want to be with Ben and I did not bring any spare clothes here anyway. So, I tell my parents politely that I want to be in my own bed. I do not want to let them know that I am going because I prefer to be with Ben tonight. My parents have each other for company.

13

FIRST BOYFRIEND HOLIDAYS

Once home, it only takes me a few minutes to quickly pack my things. I rush over to his house as I do not want to be even one extra minute apart.

When I arrive at Ben's house, we are both excited to see each other even though we only saw each other this morning.

We go straight to the drinks he has bought for the festive season. Luckily, he has coffee liqueur, so I can continue drinking where I left off. I wait in his living room while he goes into the kitchen to bring the bottle in.

We enjoy the remaining few hours of Christmas Day, drinking and talking about our family get-togethers. I assume his was more interesting than mine as it was only the three of us, where Ben, his sister, his nephew and niece and two cousins were all at his parents' house.

Ben tells me how they played board games while waiting for dinner to be ready. Dad opened a bottle of Cava for everyone and the kids had juice. His sister was accused of cheating at the game. At dinner time, his dad traditionally carved the turkey and his mum accidentally set a place for Ben's uncle. Everyone went quiet at first, then brushed over the mistake by carrying on talking about how lovely the food looked. He then went on to talk about putting a film on that was suitable for the kids. During the film, he began wishing that I was there and feeling how much he wanted to see me tonight rather than waiting till tomorrow. I can picture this family scene and it makes me quite jealous.

He asks me how mine went and I find myself telling a brief description of drinking and watching television before dinner. Then I talk about my parents asking me about him. Ben is intrigued to know what I told my parents.

I tell him that I told them we are boyfriend and girlfriend and how long we have been together. Ben's face lights up when he hears me telling him about the conversation. After I finish telling him the two-minute story of my day, he stares at me.

I give him a bemused expression, 'Why are you looking at me like that? I only told you about the most boring Christmas.'

Ben still stares at me, expressionless, and says, 'You are so gorgeous. Even when you tell the simplest of stories, I can sit here and listen to you.'

I try to laugh off what he said thinking he is simply being nice. 'I enjoyed my time with my parents, but my day sounds boring compare to yours.'

Ben sounds like he is being kind. 'Trust me, my day was not that exciting compared to yours. I felt overwhelmed with all my family there. I mainly sat and watched.'

We end up cuddling each other while we are still sat on the floor, using the sofa cushions to support our backs. He accidentally leans his hand on my stomach which makes me wince a bit. I try to play it down but he notices my expression of pain. He apologises quickly and I tell him it is okay.

We start to kiss again but my tummy is playing up after he briefly leant on me. I ignore the dull pain as we embrace.

This is the best Christmas ever.

WE HAVE BEEN inseparable since Christmas night. We have been taking it in turn staying at each other's home.

I am enjoying my time off work, sorting out domestic chores such as cleaning the apartment and washing clothes. I am expecting Ben to come round for about seven, straight from work after catching the train back to Milton Keynes.

I HAVE NOT HAD any more hallucinations since my episode in class. I feel relieved that it was only a phase.

I HAVE dinner on the table when Ben arrives. I feel like we are an old married couple. I made us some baked chicken thighs seasoned with herbs and mixed vegetables. I also brought home some mini cheesecakes from the super-market for dessert.

Ben is grateful and moans at me for going to so much effort. He had plans to either cook for me or order takeaway. I shrug and tell him it is done now. He gives me a peck on the lips to show his appreciation and we sit down to eat.

He tells me how his day in court was while I tell him how domestic I was at home. We make each other laugh with the way we tell our days. Moments after I take the plates away into the kitchen and get dessert, I see a squirrel again out of the corner of my eye. It is stood upright simply staring at me. I pretend it is not there and walking into the kitchen and place the plates by the sink.

As I PUT the plates down on top of each other, I see the squirrel standing on the window sill above the sink. After a while of staring at each other, I put my hand out to touch the squirrel. I have a nervous smile as I move my hand towards it. My fingers go through the squirrel's tummy. The squirrel does not react and keeps staring at me. I take my fingers out of its stomach. I try to make the image go away by blinking and then closing my eyes for a few seconds. It has not gone away.

I suddenly realise that I have been away a while and I am worried that Ben will come in and see what I am doing. I quickly gather myself and as I am about to go back inside, the squirrel vanishes.

I BRING our desserts on side plates into the living room. I thought Ben was going to ask why I was so long, but he does not mention it. While we eat our desserts, Ben asks about what I want to do tomorrow for Boxing Day. My mind is blank and I would be happy to stay in and chill out. I tell Ben that I have nothing in particular and that it would be nice to stay in and be lazy.

As we finish our cheesecake, I see the squirrel again in the middle of the living room staring at me. I stare at Ben, pretending that I cannot see it. Ben is still oblivious to my imagining animals in my room.

14

HOPES AND DREAMS

It is a couple of days before New Year's Eve. As I wake up alone in bed, I start to think about how my relationship is going. Ben went to his own bed as his house is a mess. He knew that if he woke up with me, he would not be asked to go home merely to tidy up. I said I would go to his house so he sticks to his chores rather than rushing over here to be with me.

I plan on going round to his about ten o'clock. If he is too slow, I will give him a hand so the day is not wasted cleaning the house. I want to go into town for lunch and do a bit of shopping.

We have not had an argument yet and I cannot imagine us having one. We get on so well that I cannot picture how an argument will materialise. I know that it is not healthy to never argue, but they should be constructive.

I have heard from old friends at college that makeup sex is great but my thoughts are that the issue is not actually resolved. So, I would not like it if Ben's attitude to resolving an argument was down to having sex. I will not use sex to resolve our differences.

Hopefully, we can have an argument soon so that I can see how he deals with confrontation and if we can work as a team to resolve the issue. I want a long-term partner I can work with through the bad times as well as the good.

I have witnessed the downfall of too many relationships among my friends to strip out the important parts of having a relationship.

I wonder what it will be like to be in love with Ben as I have no idea how it feels. My current senses tell me that I really want the relationship to last and do not see it as an experiment for a future partner. I want to go to bed with him every time I see him, so I guess it is lust at the moment. I am not thinking about moving in or making short-term plans yet. I wish there was an instruction manual on how to conduct a relationship and the signs of when you are in love. It would make life so much simpler.

Ben has organised for us to go to a house party hosted by one of his friends. It will be the first time that I have met his friends. This tells me that we are officially a couple, even though we agreed to be mutually exclusive. Even though we have been together for only six weeks, it seems like six months. It gives me extra reassurance that we are together and this is not a five-minute fling.

I know that it sounds silly, but I guess I am learning new things about myself that I never knew. I was once told that when you are in a relationship, you learn about yourself rather than about the person you are with.

ON A SEPARATE NOTE, my hallucinations have become more frequent since Christmas evening in front of Ben. It will get to a point when he will notice and I will have to try and explain my issue. But until then, I will simply live with it, hoping it is still a phase.

I am hoping by then, we will have been together for three months. Hopefully, even though it is unrealistic, Ben will have been with me long enough to cope with whatever the outcome is. I think a minimum of a year is more realistic for a boyfriend to be willing to cope with a potential life-changing illness.

I wonder how I would react if Ben had a long-term illness. If I am honest with myself, I do not think I would handle the news. I assume I would struggle with being a carer for him. Because this is how I think, I assume that Ben will not be prepared to look after me. I would like to think he would, but how could I expect him to, if I am not able to?

By the time I finish having these thoughts, it is after nine o'clock and I have fifty minutes to get ready.

DURING MY SHOWER, I remind myself of the time Ben and I were in here pleasuring each other. It puts a smile on my face as I think about it more. I wish he was here now so we could repeat what we did. After I finish in the shower, Ben calls me as I am drying myself and I answer his phone call. I tell him that I am drying myself and so I have to speak on hands-free. Ben jokes with me about wishing he was here to watch me. He tells me that he would like to help me by ensuring the crevice of my bum and vagina were thoroughly dry, and make sure I cleaned my breasts thoroughly.

I TELL him to stop being silly and sigh at him. I change the conversation abruptly and talk about what our plans are for today. Also, I want to know more information about the New Year party in regards to his friends and how many people I am going to meet for the first time.

Ben mentions that I will be meeting ten of his friends from college and that there will only be about fifteen of us. It makes it more comfortable knowing that it will not be a big crowd of people to be introduced to. I am excited about going to the party and being introduced as his girlfriend.

Ben tries to play it down to make me feel comfortable about going. I make it clear that I am totally comfortable with meeting his friends. He even asks me when he will be introduced to my friends. I have not even thought about it. At best, I can cope with holding a relationship down and going to a job. I tell him that I have four best friends who are all married, so it is not that straightforward to introduce them to him. I would have to introduce them individually and most likely at their houses. Ben is completely happy with that and there is no pressure to organise a meeting with my friends. I tell him that I cannot wait until he meets them.

We realise what the time is and I tell him that I want to get off the phone so I can get round to his house as soon as possible.

WHEN I GET to his house, I can see that he has managed to tidy up. We plan on leaving in the next hour. I assume that we will take a breather and catch up with ourselves. But we end up having a quickie before we go out for lunch.

We cannot help ourselves; we start kissing and giggling about how we have the urge to do it spontaneously. As we struggle to take our own clothes off and find it hard to unlock lips, I wonder if I am playing catch up through having no sex in my teens, twenties and early part of my thirties. We decide to be adventurous and do it on the living room floor. I think about the potential carpet burns and suggest putting down a bedsheet. As the words come out of my mouth, I immediately feel I am being a prude. I laugh seconds after what I said, feeling embarrassed, but he is sweet and runs into the kitchen to see if there is a dry bedsheet he has recently washed. He throws it roughly on the carpet and simply lies there naked, on his back, with open arms. I find him funny and kneel between his legs and start giving him a blow job.

I have gained confidence in giving a satisfying blow job and he cums every time now. It is only because I have listened to his quirky noises and his breathing. He always makes me cum now he knows what I like.

He loves it when I swirl the end of my tongue around the tip of his penis as it focuses on his sensitive spot. The moment he cums, I always get startled when he squirts against my upper lip and it sometimes goes up my nose. I can never get used to the initial ejaculation.

After I make him cum, he motions me to get on my knees and hands as he wants to enter inside me from behind. I nod my head with enthusiasm and get into position. I feel him even more and groan as I appreciate the feeling.

He goes gently at first, but I want him to go a little faster, so I reverse onto him at the pace I want. He soon understands and I feel his hands on either side of my waist as he holds me still and replicates the pace. His pounding means it does not take long before I cum on his dick. It surprises me how little time I took to reach orgasm. Ben wants to continue and so I let him, as I can easily see myself cumming again. After another few minutes, my body tenses again and I uncontrollably shake my right leg. I collapse on my stomach and he continues to ram into me. The feeling is even more sensual as he builds up speed and I hear him groaning above my head. After a few minutes, I feel his cock twitching inside me which I have never felt before. He feels bigger inside as he is close to climaxing a second time. I find myself sticking my bum in the air so I can feel more going inside me. Ben gives a loud scream as his body stiffens against my bum and lower waist. He then collapses on me like a sack of potatoes.

WE LIE in a heap recovering from our session. I thought I could not enjoy sex anymore. That was amazing and I loved every minute of it. I begin to giggle in astonishment and Ben soon joins in the laughter.

As he pulls out, I realise how sensitive I am still and shudder a little. I glance down and see how much of a mess we have made on his freshly cleaned bedsheet. I notice his cock has a glistening sheen of my love juice. I cannot believe I came that much. That has to be my favourite position now.

We have a shower together and, luckily, my original clothes are not soiled by my sweat and cum, so I am able to change back into them and not feel dirty.

We have worked up an appetite for lunch and go to a pizza restaurant in Milton Keynes shopping centre. Ben drives us into town.

While we are eating, I have my hallucination of the dancing squirrels, which is now becoming normal. It is a part of my DNA now. It is like being able to see someone in the corner of your eye making funny faces at you and you are aware of it, but you choose to ignore it so the person will eventually give up as it is not having any effect.

Ben is a great distraction; I am admiring his gorgeous face and focusing on him now, to drown out the noise my mind conjures up. I listen to him intently and react to his conversation on who will be at the party.

Every time I use the toilets, I cover my ears and close my eyes until I am finished and then hum to myself until I am back with Ben.

After we finish our main and dessert, we go straight to our choice of clothing shop. The noise of rustling shopping bags, footsteps and indistinct chatter drowns out the occasional voices inside my head.

The afternoon goes quickly and it is dark by half-past four. While we head back to the shopping centre car park, we think about what to do tonight. I tell him that I want to stay in and prepare a meal. He agrees and we decide to go to a supermarket and find inspiration for what to cook.

WE FINISH BUYING the items for our meal and arrive back at Ben's place, where we relax for a while before cooking. We cook together this time which I find therapeutic.

I prepare the vegetables by washing them and cutting them into strips or quarters. We are eating broccoli, carrots and swede. We bought a leg of lamb and Ben is cleaning it and seasoning the meat.

I partially boil the vegetables so they are almost soft; then I can roast them. They taste sweeter that way. Ben pours out a glass of wine to drink while we are cooking. He also pours some of the wine over the lamb to add flavour to it.

We also have low music playing from a national radio station that is still playing Christmas songs. There is a nice ambient feeling in the air as we work in unison. The kitchen is starting to feel hot now since we started cooking thirty minutes ago.

We cannot take our eyes off each other while we cook together at close quarters. I cannot believe we had sex earlier today in the living room. I wonder where else we will have sex. One of those places is not in the car. I do not fancy going to a secluded place and it turns out to be a dogging area. I would rather do it in the car outside his house. At least we will know it is the neighbours watching us rather than some strangers.

BEN THINKS that he is beginning to fall in love with Sarah as he studies her mannerisms, the way she thinks and her facial expressions. He finds her quirks funny and the way she gets distracted easily by things in the room. He noticed that from the beginning, on their first date. He found her flickering her eyes between him and whatever was happening behind him to his right. After several dates, he now knows that that is the way she is. He would never change her. He finds that it is a part of her makeup that he likes about her.

He finds that she sometimes stares into space like she is in deep thought. But it does not bother him as she can still recall the conversation and give the correct response.

He thinks that she has an incredible body and always has the urge to want to sleep with her at every opportunity.

In his eyes, Sarah is perfect. He likes the way she wears her hair, both in a ponytail and down. He likes the way she smells and how she breathes when they are having sex. He finds her cheeks and nose cute and loves the way she kisses him gently and seductively puts the tip of her tongue in his mouth occasionally.

He could not believe that she was a virgin because she seems to have picked up how to push his buttons overnight. After only two sex sessions, she knew what to do.

He can see himself marrying her at some time way into the future, like three years down the line. He can visualise getting engaged to her even though it has only been a few weeks. He feels that, in a year's time, he will ask her to marry him and then plan the wedding for a couple of years.

He has not had any conversation with Sarah about his feelings towards her or discussed the future with her, but he feels that she will have similar feelings and ideas of the two of them together for the foreseeable future.

He wonders when they will have their first argument and how they will resolve it. He is not interested in make-up sex. He has experienced that before and the issues have never been resolved. He can imagine Sarah being very problematic and using a methodical approach when resolving an issue.

He finds that Sarah's natural body odour is more than pleasant and finds that her vagina is addictively tasteful. He never really enjoyed oral sex with his previous relationships until he met Sarah. He cannot get enough of tasting her folds and smelling her.

I NOTICE that Ben is deep in thought and not sure what he could be thinking. I would like to think it is me. It is not long now until dinner is ready. I feel that I am ready to talk about us and find out if his plans for the future are in line with mine.

He always makes me smile unintentionally when we make eye contact. Not that I am an expert on men's size, but he always brings me to climax and so that is enough for me.

While we have been cooking, I have been having my usual episodes and making myself useful in the kitchen, which has helped me to ignore it. Luckily, I am not having visions of horrible people or the devil. These animals have character and make me laugh inside. I do not know why my characters are squirrels and a garden gnome. Not sure why I am not imagining people.

WHILE WE ARE EATING our meal, I nervously bring up the subject of us. 'I know it has only been six weeks, but I was wondering where you see us in, say, six months' time?'

Ben finishes chewing before he can give me an answer, 'I think that we would still be living like this, taking it in turn to stay at each other's place. We will have introduced each other to our friends and We will be wondering if it is too soon to move in together. What about you?'

I like the sound of what he is telling me. 'Well, I can see us doing the same thing. I do not want to freak you out, but I am starting to fall for you even more.'

Ben smiles when he hears that. 'That is good because I think I am falling for you really hard.'

He makes me gush when he says that. 'Good, because I do not want to meet anyone else.'

'What do you like about me?'

I ponder on the question as I think back on our dates; 'I like the way you always ask for my opinion when making decisions. I like the way you make me laugh. You are thoughtful. What do you think about me?'

Ben does not take long to think up what he likes about me. 'I like the way you appear to drift off into your own little world, but you are still able to know what I said.'

I nervously gush, not realising that he has noticed, 'I do not mean to do that. There is a reason.'

Ben is not interested, luckily. 'I also like the way you wear your hair.'

'I have one important question that is make or break for me; do you want to have kids?'

Ben nods his head, 'Oh yeah. I would like to have at least two kids. What about you?'

I smile with delight, 'Yes. Two. Maybe three at a push. I am not bothered what sex they are, as long as they are healthy. How about you?'

Ben is honest with me; 'As long as they are healthy and do not have any disability, I do not care if they are a boy or girl. I do not have a preference.'

I only have one more question, 'Do you want to be married?'

Ben goes on; 'I do not want children outside of marriage. I have been brought up traditionally. How about you?'

I nod my head and smile with relief; 'Yes. My parents also brought me up to be traditional.'

MY HEART IS at ease now I know that he would like to have children and be married. We finish our dinner and spend the rest of the evening sipping wine in front of the television. We turn in for bed with no intimacy by ten o'clock.

A NEW FRIEND

Ben wakes me up when I hear him walking around the bedroom and the light is on. It feels nice waking up in his bed. I feel like we are married every time I wake up in his bed. It is a nice warm feeling.

Ben picks up a pair of jeans from the end of the bed and puts them on. He struggles a bit, then I notice they are my jeans. I chuckle at him and tell him that he is an idiot, before letting him know that he is trying to put my jeans on. I throw one of my pillows at him for good measure. He throws it back in my face and stares at me with a fed-up expression.

I push the pillow away from my face and stare at him as he notices that there is something in my jeans pocket. He has a curious expression as he pulls out a bit of paper. He shows disappointment as I think he thought it was cash. The bit of paper is pink and creased where I imagine it has been there for weeks. I have not worn those jeans for over a month. Ben unravels the paper wondering what it is and says out loud that it is a lottery ticket.

I frown, wondering why there is a lottery ticket in my jeans pocket. I shrug my shoulders at him, not having a clue why that was there. I double-check if the jeans were his and question why he buys lottery tickets. He has never bought them with me and I have never seen tickets around his house. He laughs at me saying that it is not him as he does not believe in wasting money on low-odds outcomes. He even starts to get defensive as I push him to admit that it is his. I think this is going to be our first childish argument.

Ben shakes my jeans at me to show me that it came from my jeans. The penny drops when I suddenly remember the time when I went to get dental floss. I remember being forced to buy a lottery ticket to make the spend up to five pounds. I explain to Ben why the ticket was in my pocket and he is perplexed. He cannot believe that I was made to buy a ticket to make up five pounds.

I find his question amusing; 'What would you have done?'

'I would have bought ten packs of chewing gum or a few chocolate bars.'

Thinking back, I wish I had done that. 'Wish I had already been going out with you. You could have saved me the money.'

Ben stares at the paper and then at me. 'I assume you have already checked the numbers and not won anything.'

I know that my luck is not that great, so I just say, 'No. Obviously, I have not won anything. I am not that fortunate.'

Ben puts the ticket in his top drawer within his T-shirts. 'I'll leave it here. At some point, I will check it. Might even win five pounds. Get the cost of the ticket back.'

'If I win ten pounds, it can go towards our next dinner date out.'

Ben makes sure that he does not let the ticket get lost by moving it to his least used drawer that has summer tops in. He makes a point of making sure I know where it is myself. Then we start getting ready for the day and prepare for the evening party. We want to bring drinks and snacks to the party.

We already have the new clothes we bought yesterday.

WE ARRIVE at the party at seven o'clock. I am wearing a green dress that is vibrant in colour. The dress covers my shoulders and is knee-length. Ben helped me to decide on the dress. My shoes are a pair of dark green plastic flat shoes. Ben is wearing a pair of dark blue Chino trousers that I persuaded him to buy. He bought a single-button dark red shirt with a sheen on it. To go with the outfit, he is wearing dark brown leather shoes, which were not my choice.

The friend who is holding the party lives in a new-build estate at Fair Fields. They live about a quarter of a mile into the estate, closer to untouched fields. His friend has a three/four-bedroom townhouse. I wish I could afford one of these homes.

We bring with us two six-packs of beer and a bottle of vodka. We also bring a couple of large single packs of chilli crisps and chicken flavour crisps.

We are one of the first couples to arrive and there are only eight of us. Only three of his ten friends have arrived so far. They are a mixture of men and women.

WE ARE all congregating in the kitchen and a couple of the guests are emptying crisps and chocolate into bowls. One of the women is unwrapping pre-prepared celery and carrot sticks. There are plenty of litre bottles of fizzy soft drinks. The other guests have also brought vodka, coffee liqueur and gin, so there is more than enough for the host's fifteen friends.

Ben introduces me to them as his girlfriend, which makes me feel happy inside. His friends, Peter, Mike and Sean, are a similar age to Ben and me, thirty-three.

PETER IS about my height at five foot five. He is of stocky build with long straight thick black hair not that far past his shoulder. He is Caucasian with lily-white skin. He appears shy as he holds his bottle of beer up at me to acknowledge Ben introducing me.

MIKE APPEARS VERY confident and friendly in comparison. He is Caucasian as well, with yellow blond hair. He is slim with long hair down to his shoulder. He has parts of his hair from the side tied back behind him. He is a little over six feet tall. He smiles at me and shakes my hand.

SEAN IS SLIGHTLY on the heavy side, standing at roughly six feet tall. He has short black hair, shaped like a crew cut. He is also Caucasian with a shadow on his face. He shakes my hand and smiles as well.

SEAN IS the one who is holding the house party. Ben has not met the other five people before and so they are strangers to both of us. We introduce ourselves as a couple and start making conversation among ourselves.

There is music playing in the living room that can be heard in the kitchen. It is mostly hit songs from over the past year playing on a docking station. There is certainly a party atmosphere. I cannot stop glancing at Ben in the corner of the kitchen, smiling and quietly laughing with Peter and Mike. Sean is busy still placing the food out in the living room.

One of the girls automatically pours out a glass of wine for me while chatting to the other four guests. It is a nice feeling having a boyfriend on New Year's night and I am excited about seeing the New Year in with him. I was told that how you spend your New Year's night will be how you spend the rest of the year. I want to kiss Ben under the mistletoe when the clock chimes at midnight.

I get asked repeatedly how we met and how long we have been together, as well as what we do for a living. They find my job fascinating, asking me for my opinion on how many planets I think there are in space. They also ask the common question about my thoughts on whether there are other life forces in the universe. I give the same answer; that I believe there are other beings on other planets. I tell them that we have simply not met them yet. They do not contradict me or mock my belief. They agree with my theory on the basis that we cannot be the only people in this universe.

Ben is finished catching up with his friends and comes over to join us as he holds me in his arms from behind. He checks to see that I am okay and settling in. I introduce my new-found friends to Ben, trying to remember their names without coming across as condescending. One of the names I cannot remember and she prompts me by saying it herself.

THE PARTY IS in full swing when the remaining seven arrive individually. Ben introduces me, proudly, as his girlfriend. The music seems to be louder than earlier. I check the time on the wall in the kitchen from the hallway. It is now after ten o'clock.

I notice that there is an additional person here that I had not noticed arrive. He is standing by himself and not attempting to interact. I find it odd as I survey the room and no one is aware of him. So, I go up to him to make him feel welcome.

HE IS Caucasian and about my height with a thin frame, like a gust of wind could blow him over. He has brown hair which is straight, short and unkempt, with a short fringe. He has a round face with a pale complexion. He appears to be in his twenties.

He comes across as timid and not wanting to be there.

He is wearing a black tank top with a white short-sleeve shirt and grey trousers.

I feel sorry for him and decide to make conversation to make him feel welcome.

I stare at him with sympathy and ask, 'Are you by yourself?'

He nervously glances at me; 'I do not know anyone here. I am too shy to go up to anyone.'

I give him a welcoming smile; 'Well, I am here. I did not know that there would be sixteen of us. My boyfriend told me that everyone was here now.'

He has a nervous voice, 'I came last minute. My name is Paul.'

'I am Sarah. How do you know Sean?'

Paul is puzzled.

I get startled when Ben touches me on the shoulder and turns me round. Ben has a concerned look on his face.

Ben's voice goes quiet, 'Who are you talking to?'

I feel worried now, 'I was simply having a moment to myself. Feel a little tipsy.'

Ben holds my hand. 'I thought you were talking to someone. You want company?'

I squeeze his hand, 'I am fine. I want your company.'

I feel I am losing myself, now I am seeing a person, not just seeing talking animals or pottery. I am keen to make that appointment to find out about my blood results.

IT IS ONLY a couple of minutes away now till New Year's Day. I managed to think up something to explain why I was staring at the wall. Luckily, there is a mural of photos in a frame on the wall and told him that I was thinking out loud. I randomly pointed at one of the pictures to explain why I was talking to myself.

We make sure that we are not apart while waiting for the clock to change to midnight. One of the guests switches on the television to see the London Eye and the Thames.

Ben and I watch the programme where a solo artist has not long finished singing one of his top ten chart songs to a small crowd. They do this every year. The presenter is coming on screen to start the count down towards the new year.

Ben and I are glued to the television to see the beginning of the count down from sixty-seconds. We get ready to kiss as we embrace each other. The timer on the top right corner of the television screen reaches ten-seconds.

Everyone in the living room starts shouting out the last six-seconds at the television screen. Then Big Ben chimes and the fireworks are set off at the same time. Ben and I kiss each other awkwardly as we time it with the chimes sounding. After a few seconds, we settle into passionately kissing and I do not want this moment to end. We block out the shouting and jeering of the other guests as we focus on us. I can taste the alcohol on Ben's tongue as I briefly slip my tongue in his mouth.

I can hear 'Auld Lang Syne' coming from the television.

This has to be the best New Year party and I cannot wait to see what the new year will bring with Ben. I can see us making long-term plans and spending the rest of my life with him.

BY TWO O'CLOCK in the morning, we are ready to go back to his place and go to bed. We are both tired now and have had enough to drink. Ben uses a taxi app on his mobile to book a taxi for now, but because everyone else is getting a taxi, waiting time is about an hour. I wish we had booked the taxi earlier, as I am flaking already and need my sleep. Ben props me up while I close my eyes as I feel drowsy from the alcohol.

· · ·

THREE O'CLOCK ARRIVES and Ben gets a phone call from the taxi driver to tell me that he is outside. We say goodbye to Sean who hosted the party. We also say goodbye to anyone we see as we head towards the front door.

When we get back to his place, we only manage to strip off to our underwear and get into bed straight away.

16

A NEW YEAR

Work starts back the day after New Year's Day. Unlike lecturers, students have four weeks off between the second week of December and the second week in January. I have to go in to prepare my lecture and classes notes two weeks before they come back.

I have arranged to see Ben at the weekend so I can work late during the week and not feel guilty. However, we are texting each other and speaking on the phone most nights, so that cushions the blow of not being able to see him during the week.

My squirrels, gnome and now a man I imagined at the party, keep me amused while I am alone working. Between the three of them, I rationalise my life and feed off them to finalise decisions in my work schedule and personal life. They have become a crutch for me and I have learnt to keep control of how I react to them appearing unannounced when I am in the midst of a conversation, activity or lecture.

I strongly believe that I have schizophrenia and it is not affecting my neurone motor skills. I do not feel that I am going out of my mind anymore. I am not causing danger to myself or anyone else. It has started to become humorous and I joke with the different characters I have conjured up.

I have consciously avoided mentioning them to my friends, parents or Ben. It is something that I do not want to be judged or ridiculed about.

On another note, I cannot wait until I have lunch with Belinda and tell her how my Christmas holiday went with Ben. Also, to catch up with her on what she has been up to.

.   .   .

DURING LUNCH, Belinda reminds me that she spent Christmas at home and her in-laws came over. The guests were her husband's parents, a grandparent and her sister-in-law. She tells me that the turkey almost burnt and smoked the kitchen out. Belinda found the grandmother annoying because she tried to turn the oven up when she was not paying attention. Also, she kept voicing her opinion on how she would make the gravy and a running commentary on how the dinner tasted. She was glad when Christmas Day ended.

When it is my turn, I tell her that Ben and I are progressing well and that we have already talked about kids and marriage. I tell her about our intimacy without being graphic about it. I feel happy and warm inside as I recollect how the two weeks off went.

Belinda is really happy for me and asks if there is anything else to tell her. I mention the time I told her about feeling ill after going out in October. Belinda remembers and I tell her that I had been taking painkillers but that I ended up going to the doctor and getting antibiotics. She is surprised that I left it that long to see a doctor about it.

WHEN WE GET BACK to work, I continue preparing my notes. My work schedule is ridiculous at this time of year as I have to also begin preparing the exam papers for May and June. I do not have any lectures this afternoon so I can focus on planning. It is not long before it is home time.

WHEN I GET HOME, Ben is so supportive as he will always come round to my apartment if I miss him too much. He will simply sit on the floor with me and talk about trivial things to keep me company. Occasionally, we will kiss if I feel that it has been ages. Our sexual activity is dampened by my anxiety about work.

I make sure I switch off from work at the weekends and we will eat out or go to his house to avoid me sitting thinking about it.

When Ben is not here at my apartment, my imagination keeps me company and I will have a glass of white wine. It sounds embarrassing but I will have a full-blown conversation with my three chums independently.

If I feel like having the squirrels to dance for me, I will watch them and laugh at their antics. The squirrels will sing any song I want to hear.

My current favourite song is 'I Believe In You' by Kylie Minogue. They are not as good as the original track but they will do. When I need a break, they will walk out in front of me. I will be sat on the floor in the living room with paperwork around me and they will dance and sing in front of my strewn work. I will move my arms and shoulders with a glass of wine in my hand. I can lose myself and switch off from work, being in my element.

The gnome helps me to discuss different ways of delivering the curriculum so it makes sense to my students. The gnome has a sense of humour and makes me laugh with his answers and one-liners. The man helps me to discuss my relationship with Ben if I have any sudden worries. He helps me to calm my insecurities. He is very good at talking through the worry I may have.

This is why I do not want to get my blood results as I am worried they will find something and drugs will make me lose my friends. I do not want my imaginary friends to disappear. They have been a blessing in my life. Ben cannot be there twenty-four seven to discuss the same issues and our get-togethers are too far apart to wait for his opinion. I prefer to discuss the issues face to face rather than trying to discuss them over the phone.

I have the best of both worlds; the intimacy and long-term relationship and company when I am feeling lonely in my apartment.

Belinda has found my quality of work to be better than before I started imagining, not that my work was poor. I have also noticed that my lecture theatres and classrooms are more packed out than ever. I am more aware in the room when I present my slides and discuss the subject. I have more enthusiasm when I lecture to my students.

THE DAYS of feeling alone and not having any friends around me constantly have gone. I have Belinda for lunchtime chats and Ben at the weekends and an evening mid-week. I must catch up with Natalie, Georgina, Kerry and Mercedes to finally introduce Ben to them.

17

I'VE GOT YOUR NUMBER

Seconds after I get home from work and go inside and switch the light on, my mobile rings and shows Ben's name. We did not arrange to call each other tonight. By the time I go to answer, it rings off. I send him a quick text to say that I need to sort a few things out and that I will call him later unless urgent. He calls soon after I send the text, so I answer this time. He is excited on the phone and I assume that he had some good news either at work or home. He is not clear on the phone and all I hear is that he has won something. I rack my brain; what could he have entered that he did not tell me about? I have to ask him to calm down and speak slowly.

He takes ages to relax enough to tell me again. He keeps saying 'won', but I am not sure whether it is a holiday, a promotion, a new client or a one-year free train ticket to work. He is still not making sense.

I end up shouting at him to shut up and collect his thoughts. The other end is quiet now and I wonder if he has been cut off. I say hello to him to see that he is still there. He calmly tells me, in between laughing, that the lottery tickets have won us some money. I ask him when he bought lottery tickets and that he told me he never buys them. He must have bought them when I was not with him during the week. I assume that it is probably a hundred pounds if he is that deliriously happy. I ask him, half-heartedly, how much he has won, suggesting a figure of ten pounds. He laughs at me and says higher. I think out loud to myself, twenty pounds. He still asks me to go higher and think big. I smile to myself and suggest a thousand pounds. He laughs again and I give up. I tell him to simply tell me. He says the words, 'Three million'. I think to myself 'okay' and suggest it must be sweets, community service, free air miles or even free shopping for life. I put these suggestions to him. He goes quiet and asks if I ever did get a degree in Astrophysics or if I actually do my job. I feel a bit insulted and bark at him to tell me. He eventually says, 'three million pounds'. I have to ask him to repeat himself. He repeats it slowly as if I am thick, 't-h-r-e-e m-i-l-l-i-o-n pounds', 'three million pounds'. He asks me if that is clear enough.

I feel jealous of him and wish I could win three million pounds. My first thought is that he is going to dump me for a prettier and sexier girl. I imagine him giving up his job and moving halfway around the world with women hanging off his arms. I am going to be left behind. Not that that is my sort of thing.

As I am thinking the worst of him trading me in for a younger model in their teens, I hear Ben squawking down the phone at me. I keep hearing him saying that it is my ticket. I correct him by saying that I have never bought a ticket. I know that I will never win anything on those things. It is a great waste of money for me. I do not even have money to waste like that. He reminds me of the ticket that the shopkeeper made me buy. But I think back and that was like two months ago. Ben is confused. Ben keeps telling me that it is the ticket I bought.

I tell him that if it was my ticket, I would have had a phone call from the lottery people. These things do not happen to me. So, I tell him he has completely messed up.

But Ben keeps telling me that we have won the three million pounds and I keep telling him that it is not we, it is him. Ben then says that he is coming over to show me. I think about all the chores I have to sort out and tell him that he cannot come round now.

Ben ignores me and hangs up. I think to myself that I do not need him rubbing it in that we are over. It is now that I need my three friends to support me.

TWENTY MINUTES LATER, Ben comes over and I open the door nervously, picturing how he is going to dump me.

HE RUSHES through the door before I have a chance to try to kiss him and say hello. He asks where my laptop is and finds it in the living room before I get a chance to tell him. He knows my password from us ordering takeaway or buying cinema tickets. He spends a few moments tapping away on my laptop. After he finishes tapping away, he turns the screen to me. I see the background logo of the lottery company. I ask him why he is showing me this. He touches the screen with his fingers.

.   .   .

HE BABBLES ON, 'You know when I found the ticket in the pocket of your jeans and you accused me of gambling?'

I have to rack my brain as to when we had that conversation; 'Ah yes. I remember. You blamed it on me that it was mine.'

Ben appears upset with me; 'It was your ticket. It was always your ticket. It was in your jeans pocket, not mine. Remember?'

My mind is playing tricks on me. 'They were your jeans. You even put them on.'

Ben huffs at me; 'And I could not get them on. I took them off and realised they were yours. You told me that the shopkeeper made you buy the ticket to round up to five pounds. You made a point of moaning about it?'

It is slowly sinking in for me. 'So, those numbers are mine? Numbers that the shopkeeper chose. I was agitated that day and simply wanted to get home. If I have won, why have I not had a letter or phone call?'

Ben is getting frustrated with me, 'Are you really a .... Did you just make that up to impress me? I cannot make it any clearer. You - have - won - three - million - pounds. I went into my drawer to get a T-shirt and saw your ticket fall out. I thought it was a screwed-up piece of paper, wondering how it came to be there. Then I remembered that I put it among my tops in the drawer. I thought I would check if you had maybe won ten pounds. When I put the numbers on the website, I had to take three or four glances, thinking the website was having a funny moment. I even phoned to confirm the numbers. They checked the numbers and verified they are winning numbers. They even reached out in the press and media.'

I have to sit down and assume I am imagining this. I keep pinching myself as I feel I have finally lost the plot. I keep expecting one of my imaginary friends to tell me that it is all a dream. At the thought of embarrassing myself, I touch Ben's arm to check if he is really here. I sense Ben is curious as to why I touched him like that. Before I give him a chance to ask, I tell him that I need to open the window for fresh air.

My next thought is how to collect the money. Ben suggests that we take sick leave and contact National Lottery tomorrow. He also offers to stay over tonight so we can contact them first thing tomorrow morning.

I need a drink, so Ben offers to pour it for us, He can only find leftover liqueur and we drink that. The more the evening wears on, the more it sinks in and the more I go giddy thinking about it. I tell myself that I only won because the shopkeeper made the numbers up. If it was me, there was no way I would have won ten pounds, let alone three million.

We end up going to bed after eleven and it feels like we are going on holiday tomorrow. It does not feel like a weekday.

. . .

THE NEXT DAY, I think about last night and it feels like a dream. I turn over, expecting to see Ben next to me, but he is not there. It startles me as I genuinely believed that last night was real. I start to panic as I now know it was another hallucination and now it is including Ben.

I suddenly hear a flush from my bathroom next door and wonder if it was my imagination. Then Ben walks in only wearing a pair of elasticated boxer shorts. Phew! I was not dreaming about Ben sleeping over; he was there because of the lottery ticket.

Ben climbs back into bed and gives me a gentle hug as he spoons me. Even if I imagined winning the lottery, nothing can make this moment feel any better.

Ben has a croaky voice when he talks near my ear, 'So, what are you going to do when it is confirmed that you are a millionaire now?'

I now have my confirmation that I was not imagining the conversation. 'Phew! I thought I was imagining last night. I didn't know what to say just now.'

Ben giggles and shakes both of us, 'I know. There is something that I want to tell you. I don't want you to say anything.'

I know what he is going to say, 'I really like you. These six weeks feels like a year to me.'

BEN GOES ON, 'We have only been together a little over a month now. I know we both really like each other, but money changes people, so, if you wake up in a day's time, a week's time and you have changed your mind, it is okay. I have no regrets about getting to know you. You made me start to believe in women again.'

I turn to face him. 'No. I like you so much. I am not going to lie. I have no idea what love is. I wouldn't have a clue if I was in love right now. All I know is that I would rather be single through this journey than be with someone else. You can bet on me.'

Ben smiles at me, 'Yes, and as your lawyer, I will make sure that your money does not go awry.'

I smile back; 'Yes. You are my lawyer. Have you ever slept with a millionaire?'

Ben is sarcastic; 'Of course. I slept with one only last week. It happens to me on a regular basis.'

We both start laughing and we start getting intimate. I miss this. It has been a couple of weeks since we made love. Ben reaches down to my crotch and starts stimulating my clitoris and I part my legs to give him full access. We know every inch of each other's body so well now that it does not take long to orgasm. I can feel how solid he is as he presses against my thigh during foreplay. I grab his solid cock and stroke it up and down through my palm. He is so aroused that he cums almost instantly, as I feel warm liquid dribbling down my wrist. I wipe his cum against his tummy. He enters inside me so easily as my vagina is nice and wet. God, I miss his cock.

It feels so weird being a millionaire that I struggle to comprehend it.

AFTER WE MAKE LOVE, we get in the shower together and then get changed together but we cover up with our towels. We smile at each other as we change.

I go into the living room to bring up the website to see the draw throw up the winning amount again. It keeps saying three million pounds. I check where the commas are, expecting them to be in the wrong place.

I tell Ben that we should verify the win first and then pull a sickie, so we do not waste a sick day over a wrong assumption. I tell Ben to call as I am shaking again as I raise my hands in front of me. Ben is relaxed and calmly phones them again. It takes seconds to get confirmation, which he gets through his mobile on loudspeaker. I am talked through what happens and told a summary of what the procedure is. As the amount is over fifty-thousand pounds, I do not have to go to any National Lottery retailer to officially confirm. Normally, I would need to get what they call a 'Win Receipt'. The lottery machine scans and validates the winnings and produces the 'Win Receipt'. The lady on the phone tells us that because it is more than fifty-thousand pounds, we contact the National Lottery company in person on the phone number Ben rang. If the winning was less than fifty thousand, I would be able to claim the money over the counter at a post office, then have the money transferred into my bank account. I am relieved that I do not have to go back to the shop with the annoying shopkeeper. Also, we do not have to get into the car and crash it from the excitement.

The lady tells me that the next step is to fill out a prize claim form that I can complete online. I also have to show proof of my age, confirming that I am over sixteen. I decide to scan my passport as proof of age. I also have to scan a letter with proof of address and one of those choices is a bank statement. So, I quickly hunt for the latest bank statement that has come through the post. Then I have to write my bank details down to have the money transferred electronically. It also asks me to fill out the 'Retailer Publicity Agreement' section to publicly advertise the win. I leave it blank as I do not want anyone to know except for my family and friends.

The form has to be printed and filled out. The form asks for full name and address. I then have to write down my preferred telephone number and so I use my mobile. Ben has to countersign the form as a witness. The lady finishes off by telling us that we need to claim it in person rather than posting the form off because it is over fifty-thousand pounds. We ask where is the nearest place we can go to. She tells us that she is checking on her computer and asks where I live. I give her the town rather than the exact address.

After a few seconds, she tells me that the nearest National Lottery regional centre is Birmingham. I go on my map app to see roughly how far that is. It is a little over an hour away. We will certainly be able to drive up there today to hand-deliver the form.

WE PUT the address in the satnav that Ben has in his car. Once the address is put in, we head up to Birmingham.

While we drive up, we both nervously tell our employers that we are unwell and blame it on a cold.

THE JOURNEY there was straightforward and they had their own car park, so we did not have to pay for parking. The visit was surreal; they saw it as just another day with someone winning. They offered us champagne so we both had a glass. Ben only drank a little as he is driving back.

They treat us like we are special but we only want to deal with the paperwork and then head home and wait.

The designated person dealing with us suggests that we open a private account and not use the account I supplied. They organise with specialists at the bank I use to open an account for winnings. All this is overwhelming for us. Ben holds my hand the whole time and any legal terminology is explained to me by Ben in plain English.

When the account is open, I will get the money within forty-eight hours. We reiterate that we do not want any publicity as we are not like that. The account will be available to use before the end of next week and the money will be in the account shortly after.

After a couple of hours, we drive back to my place. We are both dazed by the visit. It still has not sunk in what has happened. All I can think of when we get back is have something to eat and talking to Ben about what happened today.

AS WE WALK through the front door, we both sigh at the same time and take our coats off. I ask Ben if this is real. Ben raises his eyebrows and exhales as he repeats my question. Then Ben asks me what I am going to do about my job. It is not like working in a fast-food restaurant where it is a no-brainer to quit your job, so it has never entered my mind before. I have a professional career and so I will find it hard to simply give it up. Ben agrees with me as he would think the same for his job.

He makes us a cup of coffee and we sit in the living room, staring into space.

I ASK Ben to stay over as I do not want to be alone tonight; I also feel he is a part of the same journey and that we should be sharing it together. Ben says that he will go and get fresh clothes but I tell him that I might as well pack and stay at his rather than doubling back.

Ben helps me to pack because I am dilly-dallying about while still being shocked by the whole thing. In the space of twenty-four hours, I find I have no money worries whatsoever. I still think it is a dream and I will wake up eventually. If it was not for Ben being by my side, I would think I was hallucinating the whole thing.

18

PAST RELATIONSHIPS

It is the second week of January and the students are back from their four weeks' holiday break. I am back at work on Monday morning. It has been a week since finding out about the lottery win. I am driving along the A34. While I am travelling, my mind is swimming around with the thought of what I will spend the winnings on. It still feels surreal and I am expecting someone to say it is an early 'April Fool'.

The past few days have been a whirlwind. It does not feel like I have won three million pounds. I keep thinking of the man in the shop who made me top up my purchases with the lottery ticket. It has been on my mind to go into the shop and let him know that I won some money. I feel compelled to tell him, simply to let him know that if it was not for him, I would not have won. He could have merely suggested buying milk, chewing gum or special offer sweets instead of buying a ticket.

I have only told my parents and I am in the process of organising their remaining three-year mortgage to be paid off in full. I have also asked them to review their private pensions so I can top them up to an annual pension of thirty-thousand pounds each. That way, they can live comfortably with only household bills to worry about and they can go on yearly holidays.

Apart from that, I have not made plans on how to spend the money. I have no intention of giving up work as I love my job. If I was working in a non-promotional career, I would simply quit and live off the interest from the winnings.

Ben has been so supportive by reassuring me that I can do whatever I want. I do not feel that I need to do anything with the money simply because it is there. He has given me encouragement to take care of my parents and show appreciation of their support throughout my education. My parents deserve to be treated as you only have one set of parents. I already knew that but it was nice to have him voice it to me.

I tell him that I have never been abroad and asked where he would like to go, but he keeps telling me that it is not his money and it should be my decision. He keeps joking that as long it is not Antarctica, he is happy to go anywhere. He keeps telling me that if I want to go to Butlins or even Skegness, he will be as happy, knowing it is what I want. He is more interested in making sure that my decisions are my own and not influenced by my friends. I keep telling him that I value his respect and I am falling for him even more.

My gnome, squirrels and the imaginary man also gave me the same answer as Ben.

I ALMOST MISS my exit for work as I gather my thoughts. As I approach work, I start to feel anxious that I will blurt out to a colleague or my students about my circumstances. I really do not want to tell anyone. If I had my way, I would avoid work altogether, after all, I can afford to.

I have minimal interaction with anyone I come into contact with, As I know I will blab it out in a second. They could be talking about their pet cat and I will turn it around to say that I am a millionaire.

It is not that I want to brag about it, it is simply that this type of thing never happens to me, but it finally came good.

When I get to my office, I shut the door behind me quickly and stand against the back of the door. I exhale, relieved that I managed to avoid everyone. I have to get my presentation notes together for my first lecture at ten o'clock. I am so paranoid that I feel I have to check my notes to make sure that there are no words that will make me slip up. I could imagine talking about how many stars are in outer space and blurt out three million. It is so hard to switch off from my thoughts.

I have not seen my friendly hallucinations for a couple of days. I find myself missing them when I do not see them for more than a few days. They give me comfort when I am by myself at home or work.

MY USUAL LUNCH date with Belinda is about our weekends and if anything of interest has happened. Instantly, I think about the three million pounds I have won. I really want to tell her but I feel I will jinx it and cause some hiccups with receiving the money. As well as my four best friends, Belinda will be one of the first I tell.

I LET Belinda do all the talking so I do not accidentally blurt out my good news. She tells me that she is going away for the weekend. She is going to

Paris to celebrate ten years of marriage. I ask if she is going to do anything specific or take it as it comes. She tells me that they are going to follow an itinerary so they do not waste time.

SHE MAKES me jealous as I think about how I would like to go on holiday. Then suddenly, I remember that I no longer have any financial restrictions. I can go on a hundred holidays. The thought puts a smile on my face and I have to lie to Belinda that I had a funny thought. Luckily, she does not ask me to elaborate, so I do not have to make up another lie on the spot.

Belinda eventually asks about my life and I tell her that my relationship with Ben is all good and that we are still going through our honeymoon phase but we have learned how to discuss any issues we have. She is really happy for the both of us. I almost tell her that I have come into some money without thinking, but I stop myself in time.

Belinda remembers about my appendix and that she never found out what happened in the end. She asks if that is now resolved as it has been a while now. I tell her that I finished the course of antibiotics a few weeks ago now. I tell her that I am fine and I have my appetite back. I even order a pudding after our main which surprises Belinda.

When we finally finish lunch, we continue having a conversation on the way back to work.

BEN IS in the law library, at his law firm. He is researching a precedential law to support his current case. There are a few other members of staff sat at glass tables doing their own similar research. When he finishes his fact-finding, he steps away from the shelf while flicking through the book and walks backwards into a colleague.

He quickly apologises before facing the person. It is a woman he knows and he has been keeping his distance from her. He feels awkward as he smiles at her and is keen to move on.

The woman is an old flame - he had a short fling with her almost five months ago. It was a couple of weeks before meeting Sarah.

Her name is Clare and she is similar to Sarah with straight brunette hair that falls past her shoulder. She wears it down and tucked behind her ears. She is a solicitor as well and only qualified a couple of years ago. Clare is young, in her mid-twenties and finds Ben impressionable.

Clare chose to end the sexual relationship because he would not commit. Even though she is in another relationship, she still wonders if she should have been more patient and waited for him.

They were together for four months with no formal arrangement of how they saw the relationship. They simply enjoyed the chemistry they felt for each other and when either of them wanted intimacy, they would let the other person know via text.

Clare was the adventurous one whenever they met up. They have gone to parks, walked trails and driven to secluded car parks. Ben is quite reserved and easily led, so he went along with her ideas.

The relationship started to fizzle out when he found out about his uncle. He wanted to focus his attention on him and let their relationship fall to the side.

Clare is not so good at being discrete; 'If you wanted to get my attention, all you had to do was ask.'

Ben laughs nervously, 'I didn't see you there.'

Clare still fancies him. 'Still have a firm bum.'

Ben is worried that their colleagues overheard her comment, so he says, 'Not here.'

Clare does not care if their colleagues notice. 'Then where?'

Ben nervously surveys the law library to see if anyone is watching. 'You have a boyfriend now.'

Clare's feelings are stronger for Ben than for her boyfriend, so she goes on, 'He won't find out. You're single; I still like you. My boyfriend won't find out!'

Ben is alarmed by her advancement, 'No. I am more focused on my career now. I do not want complications. You are young and should be enjoying life. I want to find the right one and settle down, not have a fling.'

Clare is happy with whatever Ben wants; 'I can settle down.'

Someone at the entrance calls for Ben to have an update on his case. He welcomes his boss's interruption and says to Clare that he will catch her later. Clare watches him walk away as she undresses him with her eyes.

IT IS home time now and I give Ben a call from the car to find out what time he will be home. When Ben answers, he tells me to hold on until he gets to his desk.

BEN CLOSES the door to his office so Clare does not overhear his conversation.

BEN SOUNDS like he is distracted. 'How was your day?'

'I had lunch with Belinda as per usual. I almost told her about the lottery win but bit my tongue.'

Ben listens while walking to his desk, 'When do you think you will be ready to tell your friends?'

'Once I have access to the account and can see the money in the account, I will let my closest friends know.'

Ben is only curious as it is not his money. 'Okay. Was only wondering. Are you on your way home now?'

I notice where I am on the A34 and gauge how much further I have to travel. 'I am approaching the junction for the M40, so I should only be about forty minutes. When are you leaving?'

Ben is decisive; 'Leaving in the next ten minutes. Quite a quiet day today, so should be home by seven.'

I think of what to cook tonight. 'I will make pasta bolognese.'

'That sounds great. See you then.'

We both say goodbye.

AFTER BEN SWITCHES off his laptop and goes to leave, Clare quickly says goodbye to him to attract his attention. He gives her a quick grin and leaves. Clare is staying on, finishing her work before she goes home.

19

CAUGHT OUT

It is the weekend and, since Wednesday afternoon, my tummy has been playing up again. It is weird that the day Belinda remembers about my illness, I begin to feel a bit peaky again. It is the same pain that I had before, but it is nowhere as bad as last time. I put it down to there being some bacteria lingering about. I have not bothered to see the doctor as the antibiotics have taken care of the worst bit. I feel a bit nauseous and occasionally sleepy.

Ben is coming over late morning after he has tidied up his house and so I will ask him to take me to A&E. I want to go as a precaution, but other than that, I feel fine. Because of the way I have been feeling, we have not been intimate, but it has only been three days.

Ben calls me as I am about to go into the shower, to tell me that he has to get something from the hardware shop. He needs to replace something in his house. So, I have to wait for half an hour for him to get back. That will be enough time to get ready.

SOON AFTER I finish in the shower, I go to reach for the towel on the floor by the bath and I feel a sharp pain. It is unbelievable and I fall on the floor in a crumpled heap. I clutch at my stomach and feel myself passing out.

HAVING BEEN to the DIY store, Ben is about to leave his house heading for Sarah's. He thinks of calling her but texts her instead to let her know he will be ten minutes.

Something is bothering Ben and he cannot think why. When he left Sarah this morning, he sensed that she was not okay. He feels that he should have stayed with her but she insisted that she was fine.

He checks his phone to see if she has replied to his text, but nothing. Sarah always replies to his text; whether it is a smiley face or a 'yep', she always acknowledges his text.

As soon as Ben gets to Sarah's building, he starts to feel anxious and is keen to get up to the apartment.

HE FRANTICALLY OPENS the door and calls out Sarah's name. There is no answer and it feels like she has gone out. He checks previous texts and reads that she was going to wait for him. He goes to the bedroom and she is not there. He remembers her going to take a shower and quickly goes to the bathroom.

It is locked, so he calls out her name but there is no answer. He starts to panic; how he is going to get inside? Suddenly, he remembers that the lock has a groove to fit a screwdriver or coin. He has neither and so thinks on his feet and finds a knife in the kitchen.

He uses a dinner knife to twist the lock and open the door. He sees Sarah lying on the floor unconscious. He calls the ambulance on his mobile. As soon as he comes off the phone, he puts her phone in front of her face, to open the phone via face recognition. He then goes through her mobile address book to call her parents. He sees 'Mum' and dials it. When he gets through, he tells her that her daughter has collapsed and that he is waiting for the ambulance to arrive. Sarah's mother is grateful and she heads to the hospital to wait for her daughter's arrival.

BEN CHECKS TO see if he can find a pulse and continues to talk to Sarah as some kind of help. He starts to get panicky, thinking that she is going to die. He knows that you can die from a burst appendix and he thinks the worst.

After twenty minutes have passed, he can hear the faint noise of an ambulance. He makes sure there is no obstacle in the hallway, so the ambulance crew can walk in without struggling.

The paramedics have to use a wheelchair to get her into the lift. Ben goes on the next lift to follow them down and he goes in the ambulance with Sarah to meet her parents at Milton Keynes Hospital.

WHEN THEY ARRIVE at Milton Keynes Hospital A and E, Ben can see the paramedics are worried and thinks the worst. Sarah is rushed into theatre straight away. Her vitals are not even checked.

. . .

SARAH IS in theatre for about two hours as the surgeon can see that her appendix has burst. Any routine appendix removal takes about two hours using keyhole surgery. When they initially used this method, they realise that it had already burst and they needed to cut her open to scrape the poisonous pus from around her abdominal cavity.

If Ben had not made arrangements to come back to her apartment, she would have died within a couple of hours.

Sarah is now on the ward recuperating and her parents are with Ben by her bedside. Sarah is still under the influence of anaesthetic.

I WAKE UP, struggling to open my eyelids and feel groggy with a dry throat. I do not think I am on my bathroom floor. I do not think I am at home as the bed does not feel like my bed.

My stomach feels a lot better than before but I still ache a little.

I notice that I am in a hospital ward with a few other patients and their relatives. I cannot see any staff. I need a drink of water to ease my dry throat. There is a plastic jug to my right, on a bedside cabinet, with a plastic disposable cup.

As I go to take a sip, a nurse comes up to me to ask how I am feeling. I ask how long I have been in here. The nurse tells me that it has only been half a day and that it is almost five. She suggests that I must be hungry.

Moments after she walks off to find someone to bring a meal, my parents walk in with Ben. They quickly ask me how I am feeling and that they will get the nurse to find the doctor. I find out that it was Ben who called an ambulance to rush me into hospital. It is all too much for me to take in and I need to hear the story when I have my faculties together.

THE SURGEON ARRIVES to tell me what happened and how long I will have to stay in hospital. It startles me when he says that if it was not for Ben coming back to my place when he did, I would have died. He thinks that if I was alone for another hour, my body would have gone into shock and eventually cardiac arrest. It is better not thinking about. The thought makes me realise that life is too short and that I should be working to live and not living to work.

Once the surgeon is finished speaking, I stare at Ben, thinking he is my hero and I think I am starting to fall in love with him.

I have already been told that I must stay in hospital for a few days to recover from surgery. I cannot do any physical activities for at least two weeks. I cannot go to the gym for up to six weeks. So, I will be off work for a couple of weeks. I have to stay in hospital at least until Wednesday. I will call work on Monday morning when the university is open.

. . .

A COUPLE OF HOURS LATER, visiting time is over and the other patients are asleep or drifting off. While I lie there fully awake, my imaginary friends appear to see that I am okay. The five squirrels do a dance routine for me, to the song 'Don't Give In' by Snow Patrol. I am worried that the music that the squirrels are dancing to is too loud for the other patients. The sound in my head is as loud as usual, so I am sure the other patients will wake up.

The gnome sits next to me and sways left to right to the music. I try to sway with him but I am in too much discomfort, so only move my arms gently. The man sits on the edge of my bed watching the dance moves. I do not feel alone now they are giving me comfort.

A NURSE AT THE NURSES' station catches what Sarah is doing out of the corner of her eye. She takes another peek and can see that Sarah is in her own little world. She wonders if she is under the influence of the painkillers.

At first, she finds her amusing, thinking it is comical in a non-discriminatory way. She brushes it off and gets back to her paperwork.

AFTER THE NURSE finishes her paperwork, she glances over at Sarah, to see if she is okay and if she is still talking to herself. Sarah is engrossed in a full-blown conversation with herself. The nurse begins to get worried for her wellbeing. She takes a mental note to let the doctor know about it when he arrives moments before her shift finishes. In the meantime, she decides not to startle her or make her feel embarrassed that she has been caught talking to herself.

THE NEXT MORNING, I wake up forgetting that I am in hospital. I did not sleep well last night through being in another bed. Ben and my parents are coming to see me this morning when visiting hour starts. Last night, I was fighting sleep as I did not want to miss out on seeing my imaginary friends. But the entertainment and conversation took its toll. I did not want my friends disappearing.

AROUND TEN O'CLOCK, my parents arrive with Ben, who had driven the three of them. It is not long before the doctor arrives and checks my clipboard to see what observations were made.

. . .

HE IS an Indian doctor with a bald head, standing at five foot five. He is wearing a pair of polyester grey trousers with a grey open shirt and a brown tank top, similar clothes to the ones he wore when I last saw him. He is in his fifties with young-looking skin.

HE INTRODUCES himself as Doctor Chopra and asks if he can speak to me in private. I cannot hide my worry in front of my parents. He insists that it is nothing to worry about and repeats that he simply wants to speak to me in private. My parents and Ben quietly slope off.

Doctor Chopra is ominous; 'How are you feeling? Let me look at your stitches. Ah, coming along well. Any discomfort?'

I still feel achy, so I say, 'It is still sore but nowhere as painful as yesterday.'

Doctor Chopra appears guarded; 'The night nurse noticed that you were talking into space. Is there something that you should mention?'

I retreat into my shell. 'Um, I was only thinking about what I need for my parents to bring in.' Phew, I had to think on my feet.

Doctor Chopra does not change the subject. 'Okay. It's just that you were talking to yourself for over twenty minutes. You were dancing as well.'

I try to stop myself from going red, 'Oh, I was repeating to myself so I could remember what I need from home. It took me twenty minutes to recite all the things like towel, makeup, toothbrush. Now it is all up here.'

Doctor Chopra sits on my bed and places his forefinger in front of me, saying, 'Follow my finger. That's it, to the left and then to the right. To the left, then to the right.'

I feel like a child, as he asks me to follow his finger. 'What are you checking for?'

Doctor Chopra ignores my questions. 'Give me your hands. Rest your hands in mine.'

He moves my hand around. I have no idea why he is doing this. 'What is this for?'

Doctor Chopra gets out a medical torch that is thin and flashes the light at my pupils. He flashes the torch in my eyes twice. I think that is it, but he tells me that he wants to do a CT scan.

He makes me worried, 'What is a CT scan?'

Doctor Chopra smiles to reassure me. 'I am only doing my job. I notice that your left pupil is only slightly dilated. It is simply a check. I will book that in for tomorrow morning.'

He is worrying me now. 'So, what does dilate mean?'

Doctor Chopra does not answer my question and only tells me that he wants to find out why my left eye is not reacting as well to the light.

.   .   .

WHEN MY PARENTS and Ben come back, they ask what he wanted. I play it down by saying that he wanted to check how well I am healing, checking to see that the stitches are fine. My parents stay till late afternoon and then they leave. They have their lives to live.

Ben is great making small talk and bringing me snacks from the coffee shop. Ben tells me that he totally freaked out thinking I was dead. It made him realise how much I mean to him. It has also made me realise how much he means to me, and I dread not seeing him again.

THE NEXT DAY, Monday, I am put in a wheelchair to be taken for my scan. It is a nurse who comes for me and takes me to the purple zone of the hospital.

The room has a large machine inside. It looks like an oversized old-style television set with a circular hole in the middle. It also reminds me of a breeze block. There seems to be a single bed fixed to a solid stand. What I assume is equivalent to a bed mattress is solid black plastic and thin. It is not appealing to lie on.

I have never seen one of these before. I am not sure if I have led a sheltered life by not watching medical dramas or documentaries. My interests are naturally the stars and science topics.

The room is clinically white with a separate room that has computer monitors inside. I assume that my scan will appear on their monitors. The reason why I know there is a separate room is because the top half of the partition wall is glass, so I can see inside.

THE NURSE TELLS me that I have to take my clothes off and my mouth drops thinking that I will be lying there stark naked for all and sundry to see. She smiles and giggles at me as she explains that I will not be physically naked. She holds my hand to reassure me and tells me that I will be wearing a medical gown. I get to keep my underwear and bra on. That is definitely a relief!

She eventually tells me that her job title is a 'CT Radiographer Technologist'. I only heard 'CT' and 'Radio' and the rest goes over my head. I do not bother asking her to repeat her title.

The scan is called a CT scan and is used to highlight dense mass. I ask her what the letters C and T stand for and she tells me that it is short for 'computerised tomography'. It can also be phrased as a CAT scan and all I can picture is her using the same machine to scan cats. I know that they would not use the machine for both humans and animals, obviously.

I go into the changing room, which is like a fitting room you get in a clothes shop and change into the gown. I leave my clothes on the small bench as I don't fancy fighting to hang all my clothes on the one single hook.

I feel naked as the back of the gown has just a thin ribbon to tie it together. I find myself still holding the back of the gown closed as I walk in. I am conscious of my bum showing even though it is a woman.

Before I have my scan, she tells me more about the machine. What I see as a bed, she tells me is called a 'couch' and also referred to as the 'Table'. The hole in the centre of the machine is called a 'Bore'. The machine itself is called the 'Gantry'.

The woman explains to me that while I am lying down, the couch will travel into and out of the bore during the scan. The CT scan combines a series of X-ray images taken from different angles around my body and uses computer processing to create cross-sectional image (slices) of my bones, blood vessels and soft tissues inside my body. I ask why all the fuss of them wanting to see my insides. She explains that the images will provide more detailed information than a plain X-ray.

She also explains that there will be a banging sound which will be the magnets moving around my body. With that, I lie down on the table with my arms by my side and keep absolutely still.

The operation of the machine lasts for about thirty minutes. I know this as I can see a clock in the room to my left, opposite the separate room.

Once I am finished, I am told that I will hear of the results tomorrow.

THROUGHOUT THE DAY, my mum comes in periodically to see that I am okay and I watch mind-numbingly boring programmes on television. I perusal social media on my mobile for any interesting stories.

Ben comes to see me when he finishes work and brings flowers. They are lovely and I can see they are from downstairs.

I ask how his day has been, knowing that he cannot give away confidential information. He mentions the current case he is working on. It is nice hearing what is happening in the outside world.

I have not told him about the CT scan as I have no idea what it is for and I do not want to worry him.

I am so glad that I have a boyfriend now. I do not know what I would do if I had no one to keep me company. Ben has been really great bringing me magazines today to keep me entertained. He even brought me a magazine on space. I have no idea how he knew where to find it.

20

MOMENT OF TRUTH

It is the start of February now and I have gone through all the magazines. I have also exhausted social media. I should be going home on Friday morning. I remember the doctor said I would only be here for five days.

I called work and told them that I would not be able to come to work for a couple of weeks; almost a week in hospital and then another week needed off work for recovery. I also phoned Belinda separately to let her know what happened. She was shocked to hear what happened and was grateful for Ben being there for me. Belinda was thinking how weird it was that she had mentioned it at our last lunch and then come the weekend, it happened.

Before I know it, the same doctor comes to see me. He has a brown A4 wallet with him. He asks when my parents will next be coming in and if I have anyone to keep me company today. I stare at him with a blank face, not knowing why he is asking this.

I can only think of Mum who can come and see me now, 'My mum. She works here. You saw her two days ago.'

The doctor has a blank expression and says, 'The hospital is quite big and, unless you work in the same department, you cannot know everyone.'

The doctor wants to wait until my mum gets here. He would rather wait till I have someone before he tells me. The doctor sees a nurse and calls her over and tells her to find my mum and asks my mum's name. The nurse goes to find her.

WHEN MY MUM ARRIVES, the doctor pulls the curtain around for privacy.

The doctor has a solemn expression and says, 'I have your results. I had a second opinion. It is what I suspected but you never expect it.'

My mum interrupts him with an anxious voice, 'What have you found out?'

The doctor has a disappointing facial expression and goes on, 'There is a dark matter in the temporal lobe.'

I notice my mum's demeanour change. 'What is it?'

Without warning, Mum takes my hand. 'What did you discover?'

The doctor pulls out a black film that is an X-Ray of a skull. It might as well be a piece of art as it tells me nothing. I turn to Mum for an answer. The doctor has sadness in his eyes.

Mum has her nurse hat on as she says, 'Where do we go from here?'

The doctor shows no light at the end of the tunnel. 'I am so sorry to have to be the one to tell you. It is not operable.'

Mum turns to me and can see I have no idea what they are talking about. 'You can tell her doctor. I am here.'

I face the doctor and wait for his explanation of my scan. 'We found a tumour here. This part of your skull is called the temporal lobe. Unfortunately, we cannot reach it to take it out. It is too far in to safely remove.'

This is all surreal for me and I need more information. 'So that is what a tumour looks like. When would this have appeared?'

The doctor thinks like a detective. 'When did you first start having hallucinations?'

I go over in my head when it began; 'It was in November. When I went running. Then when I went on my first date with my boyfriend, Ben.'

The doctor shows sympathy. 'So, it is likely that you have had the tumour for the last two months.'

I need to know where we go from here, so I ask, 'So, if you cannot operate, what will happen to me long-term?'

The doctor finds the words hard to get out; 'So that you know what you are facing, I am going to tell you what symptoms to expect. Right, your visions are likely to persist and get stronger. Your short-term memory may start to go, like forgetting where you put your car keys. Your hearing may start to go and your speech may deteriorate. Each person is different. You are likely to have headaches which come on and worsen at a later stage.'

It all sounds to me like he is talking about someone else, so I ask, 'My next question. How long can someone live with this?'

THE DOCTOR GLANCES at my mum before giving me the answer; 'It is not good. Something like this will be anywhere from six months to nine months. In some cases, shorter. We cannot know for certain until we monitor it. We will know for certain by the end of February.'

I have a lump in my throat from the shock and have other questions, 'How did this happen? Is it hereditary? Would someone in our family already have had this?'

Mum shakes her head and answers, 'There has been no history in our family.'

The doctor has no answer; 'There is no rhyme or reason.'

Mum wants to know about removing it, 'How soon can you remove the tumour?'

The doctor comes across as helpless, 'I spent the last two days asking my fellow colleagues for their opinions. I was hoping that they could prove my theory wrong. I am sorry to have to tell you, it is inoperable. Your mother, being a nurse, knows that what I am saying is true, based on the scan.'

I quickly blurt out, 'How long have I left to live?'

Mum is repeating the word 'no' as the doctor goes to answer my question. 'Based on dealing with numerous cases, six months. But we need to monitor it for a few weeks to get a more accurate rate of growth.'

Mum clutches at straws as she asks, 'Chemo? That can slow it down at least.'

The doctor does not show hope, 'Chemo only aggravates it. It speeds up the growth.'

I think of my appendix bursting. 'If I had not come into hospital because of my appendix, I would have never known. One day I would have unexpectedly collapsed.'

The doctor finds my theory harsh, but continues, 'Something like that. But I would like to think that you would have gone to see the doctor because of the headaches.'

There is nothing else to discuss. The doctor puts his hand on my forearm before leaving us alone to digest it all.

Before he leaves, I ask him for his previous experience with other patients. 'What have your other patients done when they found out?'

The doctor is surprised by my question. 'Well, I do not pry into my patients' personal thoughts or ask what they are thinking. But there is one thing I have picked up since doing this job. Life is too short. I suggest you go to work, step into the centre of your office, take one long look at your office, then walk out. Close the door behind you. Get a loan. You do not by law need to tell them about your illness. And live each day like it is your last.'

I glance at Mum and then at the doctor. 'I won three million pounds.'

The doctor is open-mouthed, 'That is ironic. I think someone upstairs has a sick sense of humour. Pardon the pun.'

Mum breaks down in tears and I find myself consoling her in my arms, not knowing what to say. The doctor leaves us to allow us to digest what We have just been told. I wonder how I am going to tell Ben, my friends and work.

.   .   .

BEN IS at his desk struggling to work as he is keen to see Sarah tonight. He is haunted by last Saturday because he was going to make a quick repair before coming back. If he had bothered to fix the crack in the wall, Sarah would be dead. He keeps playing it over and over in his head. He knew that something was not right as Sarah moaned about feeling pain again, even though it was less painful. Ben feels that he should have voiced his concerns rather than relying on Sarah to take care of herself.

He senses that something is not right, so is finishing work early today so he can make the most of the visiting hours. His manager already knows his circumstances and is relaxed about him sloping off early.

Clare comes into his office to ask how he is as she has noticed him being vacant. Clare does not know anything about his personal life as he is very private. She has no idea that he is in a relationship with someone else.

Clare is concerned for him, 'Is everything okay? You have seemed preoccupied.'

Ben stares at the same piece of paper with no expression and asks, 'What makes you think I have been withdrawn?'

Clare shrugs her shoulders and says, 'You have not said a word to me all day, or been all that sociable lately.'

Ben stares up at her. 'I have had some personal things going on. So, I have been withdrawn. Nothing for you to worry about.'

Clare wants to approach the subject of them getting back together; 'If you need a shoulder to lean on, you do know I have great shoulders.'

Ben appreciates her olive branch and says, 'I will bear that in mind. What is his name?'

Clare is not sure what he means by that. 'Who, Mark? My boyfriend?'

Ben never asked what his name was before. 'Mark. Mark is lucky to have you.'

Clare sees Mark as an afterthought, 'It's not Mark that needs worrying over. I am concerned for you.'

Understandably, Ben does not feel comfortable confiding in his previous lover. 'Thanks, but I will be okay.'

Clare respects his privacy and walks out. She turns her head to glance back at him before she walks out of his office, but he does not look up and goes back to his work.

IT IS after five and Ben is already on the train from Euston to Milton Keynes. He stares out of the window while thinking of Sarah. He cannot wait till she comes home so he can take care of her. He wishes that he could have met her parents for the first time under nicer circumstances. There had been no suitable time for making their acquaintance formally. He has felt a bit left out and it is hard to make general conversation. Sarah has quite rightly focused on recovering and so has not been selfish talking about her parents. He only wants to wait until she is out of hospital and fully recovered before he discusses that. In the meantime, he will simply be as friendly to her parents as he can be.

IT SEEMS like we have been crying for more than an hour. It has not sunk in properly that I have been given this prognosis. Because I feel totally fine and have no symptoms, it feels surreal. My perspective on life has completely changed, not worrying about work or stressing about life. I feel that I have reached euphoria. Nothing scares me anymore, like wondering if I will get married, if I will have children and what my future may be. It has now been mapped out for me. I know that I will never have to think about what my future will be.

I feel at peace with myself but worried why I am not frightened of knowing my fate.

DAD FINALLY ARRIVES with some fruit and does not pick up on us crying. I wonder how Dad is going to take the news. I am worried he will take it hard and not act rationally. I am more worried about how my parents will go on after I am gone rather than caring about my own life. I guess that it is because I believe there is another life after I leave here. If I did not believe there was an afterlife and was scared, I would be selfish and only think of myself.

I guess I assume that the people I care about will not cope well with my news.

My mum looks at me to decide whether he hears it from his daughter or his wife. Either way, it is not going to make it easier for him to take the news well. However, he already senses that it is something bad by the way my mum sounded on the phone.

I do not know about myself, but mum still has signs of tears in her eyes and is making Dad suspicious. Mum stares at me and I do the same before I ask Dad to sit in the chair next to us.

As I tell my dad how the doctor explained it, my dad's jaw falls open in dismay as he struggles to digest my words. I continue to tell him in a slow, calm, soft voice so that he can take it all in. He interrupts me now and again when he hears 'life expectancy' and 'inoperable tumour'. Normally, I would be irritated but this is understandable.

BY THE TIME BEN ARRIVES, my parents have left to go home. I asked them to leave so I can tell Ben alone. I did not want to make him feel uncomfortable not being able to be himself when hearing the news. It still feels unbelievable that I am living some else's life for one day. My own life will return tomorrow. Even when I tell Ben, I feel I will wake tomorrow and this day will be a dream.

Ben walks in and asks why my parents are not here. I ignore his question and ask him to sit on the end of my bed so I can hold his hand.

A silent tear rolls down my cheek as I say, 'I am going to tell you something. I am not going to hold you to ransom. I solely want you to listen. If, after I tell you, you want time to yourself or...if, for some reason, I cannot get hold of you, I'll understand.'

Ben looks really worried. 'What have you done? Slept with the doctor?'

He makes me laugh and my stomach hurts; 'I wish.' I quickly stop laughing and repeat, 'I wish.'

Ben then stops laughing to allow me to speak; 'Go on.'

It takes me two attempts as I take a deep breath each time. 'Here goes. I had a scan on Monday morning. I didn't mention it because I didn't want to worry you.'

Ben interrupts, 'Well, you are worrying me now. Sorry.'

Another tear escapes as I explain, 'The doctor came to see me this morning. He tells me that I have something in my brain the size of a pea. Based on the scan, the doctor says that I should be getting my affairs in order.'

Ben's eyes start to go reddish as he demands, 'Tell me straight.'

I feel that I cannot tell him now as I start to cry, 'He gives me six months.'

Ben gently grabs me in his arms and I cry uncontrollably on his shoulder. He cannot stop feeling emotional as his body shudders and I can hear him start to cry.

I try to make light of it by reminding him, 'We do have three million pounds.'

Ben tries not to laugh through his tears, 'Yes, we do.'

After a while of getting over the news, Ben does not want to leave my side. He wants to stay beside me. I thought he was going to want to leave me, and I really could not have blamed him. It takes a lot to accept this situation in someone you have only been with for two months.

BEN IS POSITIVE; 'Just think, if your appendix had not burst, you would be none the wiser. You would not be able to take this opportunity to re-evaluate your priorities. I am not being religious, but don't you think something or... some god is watching over me?'

I repeat what the doctor said, 'Exactly what the doctor said. I could have been spending time with you and taking our time for granted and not making every minute count. When my tummy heals, I want sex every day. Twice a day. No three times a day. At your office, my office, in my lectures in front of my students.'

Ben starts to laugh, thinking I am possessed; 'Maybe the doctor shouldn't have said anything. Do I get a say in this?'

After we both calm down from laughing and the reality starts sinking in again, we sit there in silent reflection. I start getting emotional again and Ben hugs me while trying not to press against my stitches. It feels like I am going to prison or being deported from England in six months' time.

Ben suddenly pulls away in confusion; how did the doctor get from my appendix being taken out to a hunch about my tumour? I was not expecting him to come up with two and two not adding up. I did not think I would be having to explain about my hallucinations.

I start to go red with embarrassment; 'You will think I am a weirdo.'

Ben is confused, 'What? Tell me.'

I find this harder than telling him about my life expectancy. 'You will dump me.'

Ben chuckles, 'You told me the worst news. What can possibly be worse than hearing that?'

I cover my face to hide my face going red; 'You will only laugh at me.'

He takes my hands away from my face and passionately kisses me. 'I want to make every second count now. Don't hide anything from me and I will not hide anything from you.'

We lock eyes and the way he gazes at me is adorable. I cannot stop myself from telling him, 'I have seen squirrels dancing to random music, a fish singing on my plate, a gnome and recently, someone at your friend's party. Apparently, a nurse saw me talking to them, except for the fish, on Saturday night. I was openly having a conversation when she saw me.'

Ben is open-mouthed and in shock. 'Right, I have a nutter for a girlfriend. Can we have a straitjacket?'

I hush him and put my hand over his mouth, 'Shh. I don't want to spend the remaining six months in a nuthouse, thank you very much.'

The realisation comes back again like thunder and we both stare at our joined hands.

Ben squeezes my hand. 'I wish I could go with you. I wish I only had six months. I love you, Sarah. I loved you from the moment I saw you again in the gym. I thought you looked sexy in your gym gear; all sweaty.'

I am now open-mouthed. 'I thought I looked hideous that day.'

Ben smiles at me and says, 'Like how sexy you look now. In your gown.'

I have no idea what love is meant to be like; 'I don't... know what love is. I am hoping you can show me what love is... before... my time is up. There is no one else I would rather have by my side.'

Then Ben remembers her inexperience. 'Wow, I was your first, wasn't I? How could I expect you to know what love is if you have never been with someone before? When you get there, you will know.'

I go red again as I ask, 'Do I make you happy?'

Ben quickly reassures me; 'You think I would still be here? I would have bolted ten minutes ago!'

I reassure him by saying, 'Though I have no idea what love is, you have no idea how much you mean to me. If I could, I would choose you rather than winning three million pounds and having this death sentence.'

Ben ruins the moment by saying that he could have sex me with right now and we both start laughing again.

21

ONE STEP AT A TIME

Before being allowed to be discharged, the nurse gives me appointment dates to have my tumour measured. My first appointment is in two weeks and after that, every three weeks. I do not see the point but they want to be able to give me a more accurate prediction of my life expectancy.

I do not know if this will give me false hope that my expectancy will extend. Ben puts the dates in his phone and says that he will come with me on each appointment.

We naturally talk about who we will tell, considering I have only met his friends once, at the party on New Year's Night and due to circumstances and us only dating for two months, he has not met my friends yet.

We had no formal arrangement when to meet our friends, but now it looks like we will have to rush things to make the most of what little time I have. Having to go for scans every two weeks will magnify my time constraint. Ben is great; so relaxed and accepting of the fact that we do not have a normal relationship where we can take our time getting to know each other. I cannot afford to ignore my friends and stay cooped up just the two of us. I want to enjoy my life with everyone and not only Ben, even though he means the world to me.

WHEN WE GET HOME, Ben surprises me by having my parents at my apartment with cooked food. It is exactly what I wanted. I did not expect to see any friends as I want to tell them under different circumstances.

Ben tells me that there is a pile of post on the side and he has tried to separate them into two piles - utility bills and personal mail. There is one particular letter that stands out and the colour of the envelope makes me think it is a wedding invitation. I am too scared to open it in case it upsets me that it is beyond six months' time. I am so glad that I can get Ben to open them up for me. Dates will now be so important when deciding what social events I can commit to.

Ben is more relaxed around my parents, which I think is because he is at my place now so, he feels that he is on familiar ground. He has the respect of my parents for still being with me even though I cannot give him a lifetime commitment. Ben does not want to be with anyone else regardless of how much time I have left. It breaks my heart that I cannot spend the rest of my life with him. We are going to spend what precious time we have together as much as possible.

My parents only stay for a couple of hours and then they hug me and kiss me, embracing the moment. My parents show their appreciation of Ben for staying with me.

WE COLLAPSE on the sofa and Ben suggests getting the post and seeing what the letters are. Ben has also noticed the wedding invitation. I tell him that I know exactly who it will be from - Georgina and her partner. I have not met her partner as it has only been us girls on nights out, with no partners or husbands being invited.

Ben brings over the letters and I ask him to open them and make a point of meaning what we said in hospital. From here on in, we will not hide anything from each other. Ben takes his time opening the wedding invitation, which has a decorative coral-coloured envelope. Ben confirms that it is from Georgina and her fiancée, Freiya. Ben goes quiet when he checks the date. I can see his mind is working out if it is beyond my time. We are in late January and he reads to himself without realising I can hear him. The moment I hear August after the date, I cannot believe it and I naturally cry into my lap as I bring my feet up onto the sofa. I am sad that I will not be there for them, not sad that I will not be there to see them tie the knot. Ben is kind by rubbing my back and soothing me, helping me to get over the upset of missing their wedding.

Ben's reaction is to use this as a perfect reason for telling my closest friends, as they will wonder why I never turned up; he adds that if he was one of my friends, he would be very upset if I did not tell him about my illness. He is good for keeping things in perspective and that it is not me and my bubble.

We open the other post and the household bills are frankly the last thing on my mind. Despite the lottery win, I have no financial concerns over making sure I pay my bills before I leave this Earth.

By the time we have talked about general things and opened the post, I feel exhausted. It is only coming up to three o'clock and Ben suggests I go to sleep on the sofa for a couple of hours. He will tidy up while I have a rest. He makes sure that my dressing does not get disturbed as he puts a duvet over me.

My week at home is strange. In the day time, Ben is at work and I am left to my own devices. I cannot do anything exertive and so all I do is watch junk television. Ben makes sure he is home by six every day and his manager is totally understanding. He treats me like we are married by making sure I do not lift a finger.

We have joyful arguments about how much I feel a burden and want to contribute. He keeps reminding me by rubbing my belly asking if it hurts. And, of course, it still feels tender and I cannot pretend that it does not. So, that ends our argument.

My parents think he can do no wrong.

I have touched on wanting to meet his parents and fully get to know them before it is too late. After almost a week of nagging him, he eventually agrees but he is nervous about his parents meeting me. He is embarrassed to admit that he thinks his parents may judge us for carrying on a relationship when we know we do not have a future. We have had small arguments, which neither of us wants as we are continually conscious of the time we have left. However, we agreed that it is only for six months. It is not like we are going to get married next week and his parents are thinking we are making a lifetime mistake.

We agree that I should meet them this weekend.

I have already made up my mind to hand my notice in at work on Monday. I am confident that they will understand my circumstances and not make me carry out my contractual obligation of three months' notice. I will not waste time arguing the small print of my employment contract as I still plan on leaving within a week. I am allowing a week for hand-over. I plan on bringing in cakes on my last day. I do not want anyone, apart from HR and Belinda, to know my personal circumstances. I do not want people feeling sorry for me. I want them to treat me the same way as anyone else who is leaving. Ben said that he will make a special effort to cook something at home to celebrate my last day.

BEN HAS BEEN STRUGGLING to focus on work, understandably, trying to avoid Clare's concerns. It has been made clear to him by Clare that she is still interested.

In the past week, when Sarah was in hospital, Clare kept on cornering him when no one was around at work. She has been teasing him by tickling him, groping his stomach and, on the odd occasion, indiscreetly brushing the back of her hand against his bum.

Ben has kept his distance by trying to be around other colleagues as much as possible, making up any excuse to liaise with other people.

His colleagues found it strange that he already knew the answer but still asked for their opinion.

CLARE HAS no idea what is going on in Ben's life which makes her like him even more. Her boyfriend, Mark, is too sweet for her and she only went out with him to get over Ben. He was the only person around to show an interest. There is nothing wrong with him, but she only loves him as a brother. They moved in together within a couple of months, which was rather hasty.

Mark is quite insecure and felt, by moving in, they were more of a couple. She agreed to it so she could feel more wanted.

They have not made love in the last couple of months. They are merely co-existing and he will not bring up the issue in fear of her leaving him.

They met when they were drunk at a bar that is around the corner from several law firms and is renowned as a hangout for solicitors and lawyers. They hooked up when they realised that they had similar careers in their respective firms.

BEN IS STRUGGLING with Clare's innuendos and Sarah's countdown clock. He finds himself having to take baby steps. His brain is struggling to cope with everything that is happening and he feels that life is going by fast. If he blinks, then she is gone and Clare is not helping the situation. He is too mild-mannered to be rude to her or cause friction in the office. He does not want people to know they had a fling together. She is junior to him and he does not want people to think that he took advantage of a junior solicitor. He assumes it will be frowned upon and he wants to work towards promotion, a promotion that he is reminded that Sarah will most likely not be around to see. It reminds him even more of what else he will not be able to share that is important to him. This makes him break down and cry at his desk.

Clare peers through his office window and notices him crying. She feels she cannot ignore it and takes tiny steps to give him comfort. It takes her five minutes to walk the twenty-seconds to his desk.

When she is standing close to him, she fidgets with her fingers not knowing how to console him as a friend. Her body takes over and without realising, she throws her arms around him. She is there as a friend for the first time, not someone trying to make advances.

After a while, Ben grabs hold of her arms so she cannot let go of him. All the thoughts and anger trapped inside him can no longer be contained. He is angry with the world because, whenever he is close to someone, they leave.

He built on his relationship with his estranged uncle after reconciling their differences. His dad did not approve of his antics and so kept a distance. As soon as he heard that his dad's brother was ill, he wanted to find out for himself about his uncle. He ended up building a good relationship with him despite his uncle's faults. His uncle was man enough to know that he had brought all his woes on himself and did not blame anyone for his mistakes. Ben ended up getting close to him before finding out that he was dying.

Now he has met Sarah, he really thought he would spend the rest of his life with her. He had that gut feeling she was the one. He could not imagine being without her. He had dreams of them having children together.

He loves everything about her, such as her long wavy blonde hair, the way she smiles, the way she smells. He likes the way her nose crinkles when she finds something awful. She loves how cute her pert bum is and what a handful her breasts are. He loves the way she pulls her facial expressions when she starts to cum. He prays that he never forgets these quirky memories or any new ones.

EVENTUALLY, Ben regains control over his emotions and apologises to Clare for being so silly and crying over nothing. Clare does not question the real reason for his breakdown. Another work colleague has noticed and he comes in to check that he is okay as well. Clare motions to their colleague to go away. She does not want him to make it more than what it is. Their colleague totally understands and nods his head, understanding what she means.

Clare suggests going out to lunch and finding a quiet place to offload his problems. He reluctantly agrees but makes it clear that it is not her excuse to pounce on him. She laughs at his comment.

I GLANCE at the time on the oven clock wishing the time to go by quickly so Ben is back at home. I miss him more when I have no distractions. My tummy is healing nicely and the stitches are to dissolve naturally, so I do not have to have them taken out. I find myself walking around aimlessly trying to find more things to tidy in the apartment. I cannot wait for next week to come round, so my life can go back to normal.

I have noticed that, over the last couple of days, I have had my appetite back completely. I make myself some chicken soup with potato to thicken up the sauce. It feels great knowing that I no longer have to think about what I can eat that will not upset my stomach.

CLARE HAS SUGGESTED GOING to one of the independent coffee shops which will be quieter. Clare coaxes Ben out of his shell by talking about one of her past problems, explaining how talking about it helped her.

Ben finally tells her about Sarah and how they met. He then tells her that they only found out last week that she has a tumour. He explains that it was not the reason for going into hospital. If it was not for her appendix playing up, she would be none the wiser.

Clare is totally gobsmacked and did not expect Ben to come out with this. She wonders how he managed to bottle all this up and holds his hand to show she cares. Ben welcomes her kindness and knows she is listening as a friend. He is relieved to find someone to talk to.

They have been away for an hour and a half and start to panic that they could be in trouble. But when get back to the office, no one notices and Clare tells him that she is always here if he needs a shoulder to cry on.

WHEN BEN GETS BACK to Sarah's apartment, he checks if he smells of Clare and takes a couple of deep breaths before going inside.

I HEAR the door open and cannot wait for him to see what I have cooked for us. I checked what was in the freezer that could defrost quickly in water at room temperature. I found a joint of lamb and decided to make a roast dinner, even though it is mid-week.

I welcome him with a smile and tell him that dinner is ready and keeping warm. I can see Ben is taken aback that I am not feeling sorry for myself or putting a damper on our time together. I ask him how his day was. I find him going quiet and know that he wants to tell me something. I give him reassurance about honesty and that I really want to know about his day, whether good or bad. He makes it clear that he has a colleague who he used to date, but who is now in a happy relationship. She offered him a listening ear. I am totally okay with it and get it. I show my appreciation for him talking to someone else about it and not keeping it strictly between us. We need our friends, whether ex-lovers or not, to talk to. I know how strong our relationship is.

It helps me to understand how Ben is dealing with this and that we are both on the same path. I am more relieved than surprised or jealous that he spoke to someone else about it. It has helped him to get his head straight and communicate with me much better. The talk has also helped him organise his thoughts and get them across better. I totally feel the same way as he does; we have both had a breakthrough in unlocking our bundle of emotions.

After a long refreshing conversation over a lovely roast dinner, we are ready for an early night.

WHEN THE NEXT WEEK ARRIVES, I go to HR to hand in my resignation letter. Even though I hand-deliver it, I have still put it in an envelope. I also include the reason for leaving, so they do not try to persuade me to stay. I plan on handing it over and leaving straight away.

After I hand over the envelope to a member of HR, I turn round and go to leave but the woman tells me to wait. My heart sinks as I have to wait for her to read the letter.

I feel anxious about her reading about my cancer. She opens the letter like it is a utility bill. As I watch her read it, I wait in anticipation of her reaction. After a few seconds, her jaw drops and she clasps her mouth as she starts to well up. She looks at me as if comparing the letter to me. Then she tells me that, for obvious reasons, the normal rules do not apply. She asks when I want to leave, whether it is today or on a later date. I tell her that I would like to stay one more week so I can make a smooth handover.

She stands up and walks around her desk to give me a hug and asks how I am feeling now. I tell her that things are fine but surreal. I explain that they are monitoring my tumour every two weeks to determine how the tumour is progressing, however, they have made it clear that it is terminal and inoperable. She asks if I want her to tell everyone or keep it a secret. I tell her I do not want people to treat me differently or favour me. For the time being, I ask her to let people know after my leaving day.

The lady understands completely and immediately tells me that if I need anything, I should not hesitate to contact her.

22

FINAL WEEK AT WORK

It is my last day at work. I have been cherishing my lunches with Belinda but feeling guilty that she has no idea that today is my last day. I have not told her as I did not want Belinda changing her routine for me. But for some reason, Belinda cancelled lunch today saying she is behind on marking her students essays.

My last lecture and classes have been cancelled on purpose and the students were secretly asked to go to an unused lecture theatre to be told in private so that I did not have to struggle to explain.

I notice Belinda is quiet and in a sombre mood on the way back to university. I do not pry and assume that she is thinking about her weekend and afternoon classes. When we get back and walk across the car park, Belinda seems distant and briefly says to have a good weekend and that I would see her on Monday. I pause before replying.

I GET to my office and start packing my things. I only have stationery and a couple of paintings of the galaxy on the wall. I thought it would take ages to clear my stuff, but it took all of five minutes to old the drawers over the box and tip them upside down. It feels like my last day at school. I have no need for all this stuff.

My phone goes off and it is a text. I read it and Belinda wants to meet me at the cafeteria. I wonder if she is upset with me or has something to tell me.

I check that I have everything; the office is bare like it has never been occupied. I remember what the doctor said about taking a long look at my office.

I stand in the centre of my office and slowly rotate clockwise. I take my time, savouring every moment. I feel sad knowing that I will not be coming back to my old office. When I think I am ready to go, I close the door behind me and head to the eatery.

WHEN I REACH THE CAFETERIA, it feels eerie as I see Belinda standing in the middle of the floor. I expected she would be sitting down, with two coffees in front of her, one for herself and one for me. She has no expression on her face.

I walk towards her wondering if I have done something to upset her. As I get within a few feet of her, there is a massive roar of cheers and people shouting 'surprise'. I was not expecting a big farewell party and this explains why she was a bit quiet over lunch.

Amid the loud and incessant chatter, Belinda explains that she could not say goodbye without making a big thing about it. I can barely hear what she is saying. I suggest that we find a quiet place to talk properly.

I notice Julie is here and her presence feels weird. While Belinda and I are talking, she keeps peering over. I cannot stop glancing back at her to see if she is still staring at me. I tell Belinda that I need to get out of here so we can hear ourselves speaking.

WE STAND OUTSIDE the door of the cafeteria and, at last, we can hear ourselves think. I wait for Belinda to speak first.

She makes a couple of attempts at getting her words out; 'I will miss you so much. I couldn't face you for lunch as I would have been counting down the time I have left with you. I feel I know you and I don't know you. I have not had an opportunity to see you... getting married... and having... children. I would have liked to have found out what that would be like for you.'

I remember having this conversation with Ben. 'I already had this discussion with Ben. I think I would have been an okay mother. I think I would have let them find their own way in life and not make them follow my career or Ben's. I would have made sure that they knew they were very much loved. I would have loved to see them get married and make me a grandmother, but my imagination is good enough for me.'

Belinda listens and does not interrupt me for the first time. It is like she is hanging on every last word knowing that it will be the last. I know that she wants to hear about what my thoughts are.

I have to think carefully what I want to say, so as not to waffle or have my thoughts misconstrued.

I find myself not making eye contact as I gather my thoughts and continue, 'I am not afraid of dying. I am more scared of being alone, not having someone there to greet me or keep me company and explain how things work there. That is my only worry. And, of course, wondering if I will find my parents when it is their time.'

Belinda starts asking me taboo questions; 'Do you think you have done something in life to deserve this?'

This was a valid point, so I said, 'Oh, yeah. Not now, but before I had my operation, I racked my brain to think if I had wronged someone or something. But if I had, I would have been made aware of it. I even thought back on whether I had smoked once, or passive smoking? I know, I don't have lung cancer. There is no history in our family. My only rationale is that I have unknowingly worked out the meaning of life. I think about children who get affected by this. I wonder if children quickly work out the meaning of life and so do not need to wait a lifetime for the next life.'

Belinda asks me one more question; 'How does it feel having a tumour inside your head?'

I explain about my visions even though it is embarrassing; 'Over time, I will start to get headaches and suffer dizziness. I will start to feel nauseous. For now, I cannot feel anything and I do not feel any different. If I was not shown the scan, I would think the doctors had it wrong. It makes it harder for me to really believe because I am perfectly fine. Except for the hallucinations.'

Belinda's facial expression perks up, 'What hallucinations?'

I feel stupid for saying this, 'I have been seeing a gnome, a few talking squirrels, a fish and a man. I only see them when I have a dilemma, like finding a boyfriend, making my bucket list. Yeah, things like that.'

Belinda is intrigued; 'So, can you muster them up when you want to?'

I smile uncomfortably. 'No. Only when I worry and I need to work think things through.'

Belinda finds my situation endearing. 'You only had to ask me. I think I give better advice than your gnome and squirrels.'

We both laugh, not thinking it abnormal or absurd. We finally join the rest of the faculty staff and Belinda has told them not to make a fuss over me. She kindly told them about my reason for leaving and instructed them to leave sorrow at the front door. I had a few gifts brought for me; spa days, bath oil and scent. I sense a theme of taking it easy and not spending what time I have left worrying.

It is almost half past six and people are already starting to leave to go home; they each, in turn, wish me well. Their faces struggle to hide the sadness as they put on a brave face for me. I behave like I am leaving to go to another university to carry on my teachings. That way, I do not feel that I am making them uncomfortable or awkward. I make a point of smiling and thanking them for the gifts. Eventually, it is only Belinda and me.

.   .   .

WE WALK TOGETHER to the car park as slowly as possible, knowing that this will be the last time we see each other. We do not say anything; it is like we know what we are thinking and that we do not need to voice it.

We hug each other differently this time. I feel Belinda holding me tighter in her arms and she prolongs our embrace. I reciprocate and we do not feel that we are in a hurry to get home.

AFTER OUR TEARFUL GOODBYE, I travel along the A34 feeling surreal that this will be my last journey home from work. All I can think about now is seeing Ben tonight.

23

MIXED RELATIONSHIPS

It is now the middle of February and, naturally, I count down how many months I have left. I have an appointment for another scan next week. I am hoping the tumour has not grown and it is something I can live with. I had a couple of episodes with my three friends, which has not helped; that keeps reminding me of it.

Since I have been home, I have been unnecessarily tidying the house up before Ben arrives home. I feel like I am a housewife and I am waiting for my husband to come home so I can feed him and tell him that I have been going to the spa. It feels weird.

I have also been going on lots of walks around areas I grew up in as a child and reminiscing on my past. I have also been pondering over preparing a will so my money does not go to the government. I wonder if Ben would feel comfortable preparing a will for me.

AFTER A COUPLE OF DAYS, someone buzzes my apartment and I assume that it could my parents. When they come up and knock on the door, I am surprised to see that it is one of my old colleagues from work. I am taken aback as I hardly know her. We see each other in faculty meetings and cross paths in between lectures and classes. I am not even sure how she knew where I lived.

Her name is Julie and she is a similar age to me. We are similar in height and build but she is brunette with slightly more on top. She reminds me of my friend Kerry, but Julie is a size ten in comparison. She has similar features to Kerry which did not register with me before. Like Kerry, she reminds me of the actress, Elsa Pataky.

She has come with a food container and I feel obliged to let her in. I had plans to go for another walk and pop to the supermarket afterwards. I am hoping she is gone by two o'clock so I still have time to do both.

Before I get a chance to ask how she found me, she tells me that she spoke to Belinda and that is who gave her my address. She says that she does not want to be a burden and only came to drop off some essentials to save me going out. I find her sweet for doing this and ask her to come in.

JULIE WALKS into my kitchen and puts the container on the side and then asks how I have been. I tell her that it is still sinking in and that I am having regular appointments to monitor it. While we are talking, I make us some hot drinks and take them into the living room.

I struggle to make conversation as she is a complete stranger. I end up letting her do all the talking and nod my head in the right place. Over time, I notice that she is moving the conversation to something I can relate to. She tells me gossip about some of the lecturers about who has been sleeping with who. I had so many suspicions and she is now verifying them. I end up engaging with her and move towards closing the gap between us. I never knew about all these stories about my old colleagues. We end up laughing and sharing each other's stories. The idea of going for a walk does not interest me anymore.

I am thinking that I could hang out with Julie when she is free while Ben is at work. I ask Julie why she has the day off and she tells me that she has taken two weeks' holiday. She thought she would check on me. I ask when she is next free and suggest meeting up again over coffee at a café or something. Surprisingly, she is thinking of hanging around with me most days to keep me company. My next two weeks sound sorted now. I will really look forward to hanging around with Julie as she will take my mind off things during the days. I promise myself to make constructive plans after that when I get another realisation of my tumour. I still feel great and my stomach is a whole lot better and pain-free.

IT IS Friday already and Julie has been round every day and has helped keep my apartment tidied. We have been on walks and she showed an interest in my childhood haunts and we realised we have a couple of things in common. I wonder why we never became friends at work. She reckons that she always tried to make conversation but I was always lost in my own world. I feel guilty as she is thinking of me and, if it was the other way round, I would still not have noticed her, even after going to her leaving party.

I make sure that I pay for all the lunches and drinks as a thank you. I have not told her about my winnings. I tell her that my parents will start to support me when my last salary comes in. She was not assuming anything. She insists on paying for the next lunch.

Apart from Wednesday next week, she is coming over every day before she goes back to work. We both give each other compliments over our wardrobe, makeup and even choice of places to visit.

I HAVE BEEN TALKING to Ben about Julie a lot and he teases me that it is a bit weird and half-jokes that she has a thing for me. I think he is being annoying when he says that, so I say the same thing about him and Clare. He tells me more about how Clare has been a great listener and offered for us to go out for dinner with them. He does not like it when I tease him, but it stops him from mocking me. We have also started having really good sex again. I don't know about Ben, but I have been making up for lost time. I have never felt this much craving for making love most nights. I think Ben is dropping hints to slow down, but I am the one who is being a lady of leisure. It has come to a point where I ask him to lay there and I do all the hard work. He must think I am possessed but he finds me cute the way I am. He also assumes the tumour is changing my personality and it scares him that he is losing the old me. But I always ask him to question my old quirks to see if I come up with the same answers. That gives him reassurance

One thing I find about being given a short time to live is that you cannot afford to be an introvert. You want to exhaust every kind of experience or you may have regrets. I do not want any regrets. Ben comes round to my way of thinking but does not want to feel that he is losing me.

We are enjoying talking about both women, making comparisons between the two. Julie's efforts always outdo his Clare's efforts. It does help, though, to brighten our nights in and weekends. It is a great distraction.

WE HAVE BEEN MAKING plans for the future where he plans on taking a sabbatical from the start of March. We are thinking of going travelling and finally using the lottery money that is accruing good interest at the moment. Because he is still at work, it feels like we are only talking about it. We are not booking anything too early as we do not want to jinx my illness. We will only pay for things when we are actually ready to go. We can afford the premium for short notice.

We are finally going to share the news with our friends in a couple of weeks, including letting Georgina know why we, I, cannot attend her wedding. Woohoo; a great party pooper. I am scared of ruining her day because she is dwelling on my problems. Not that I am expecting her to, but her personality and the fact that she cares tells me that it is possible. I still get tearful when I think about it.

. . .

I GET a surprise when Julie tells me that she will not be able to see me the day before my appointment. She has unexpected plans that she does not divulge. It puts a damper on things for me but I will make the most of our last day. She wants to cook for me and drink some wine, even though it is in the day time. I tell Ben about it and he jokes with me again that she fancies me and has been priming me. I sarcastically laugh at his humour and say the same thing about him and Clare.

BEN HAS BEEN HAPPIER at work now that he has been able to talk about his sadness over Sarah. Clare has been great at encouraging him to talk to her about the fun things they have done. She has steered him away from the negative thoughts and focuses on the here and now.

Clare has been struggling to put her feelings for him aside and come across as selfless. She has not told Ben that she has ended her relationship with Mark. She realises that what she feels for Ben is not an infatuation. She thinks she has fallen in love with him.

AT THE WEEKEND, Ben and I sit down and open up an atlas to discuss and plot how we will travel the world. We plan on going in May for three months, spending two weeks at a time in each place, so I can spend the final moments back here with immediate friends and family. The countries include India, parts of Africa, Australia, North America and lastly, Ireland.

We check our list of accommodation and the various activities we can enjoy in each country. This has helped us to deal with our misfortune and has been a way of sharing our time together productively, rather than wasting it in front of the television.

TUESDAY ROLLS along and I push him to have a quickie before he gets up to go to work. Knowing I have nothing to do, despite how tired I feel, I can catch up on sleep before Julie comes round. He is not in the mood as we only had sex last night. Maybe my personality is changing because of my tumour, as it feels like a week since we had sex. I give him a blow job to make him stand to attention. I have given him so many blow jobs now since coming out of hospital, I feel I am an expert. He loves it when I slap him against my tongue and dribble saliva over his penis before slurping on it. It really turns him on and he cannot stop getting erect.

As soon I am happy with his weapon, I quickly lie on my back so he can get on top of me. It is so great not worrying about being in pain when he is on top. I love seeing his facial expression when he cums. It makes me giggle and enjoy making love with him even more. I like him being quite fast and rough now, but it has taken him a while to adjust to that. He felt like he was treating me like a piece of meat at first, but I grab his bum cheeks to encourage him if I feel he is not going fast enough. He cums a lot easier when I make him. I certainly cum in no time and I find myself digging my fingers into his back, so I now cut my nails so as not to cause him to bleed.

After our lovemaking, he struggles to walk as his legs have turned to jelly. I laugh at him and he puts his finger up at me. I joke with him that it will set him up for the day and he does not need breakfast.

When he is showered, dressed and ready to go, he gives me a long passionate kiss before heading to work. I pretend to unzip him to wind him up and he rushes out of the bedroom before I get a chance to pull it down.

I TAKE a long soak in the bath to make the time go by, while I wait for Julie to come over. She mentioned that today will be a goodbye gift. I am wondering what she is going to bring over for lunch. I kept offering to get pudding or soft drinks but she was adamant that she would provide everything.

I told Ben what is going to be happening and he thinks it is a lie. He jokes that she is only bringing herself and will make a pass at me. I told him that it is more likely that Clare will make a pass at him and she has a boyfriend.

EVENTUALLY, it is that time when Julie is due to arrive and I jump when the buzzer goes. She is a few minutes late but she texted me ahead of schedule. I open the door to see a hamper and a bottle of red wine.

She has gone to a lot of trouble. I think of what Ben said and I will text him later to prove him wrong. I tell her that we can eat it in the living room. Before we have our lunch, I make us a cup of coffee and we chat for a bit first. When we realise what time it is, we open the hamper and take out what she has brought for us.

She tells me to sit on the sofa, relax, open the wine and pour myself a glass. She makes me sit on the left of the sofa and she sits on the other side. When she bends over and reaches to take the food from the hamper, I cannot help but notice how perfectly round her bottom is from a side view as her skinny jeans outline the curves of her cheeks. I feel jealous of how toned her body is. She lingers next to me for a while not leaving me much else to look at. I take a gulp of my wine to distract myself from looking at her body. She reminds me of Kerry.

.   .   .

AFTER SHE IS FINISHED, she turns to sit back down and her leg knocks against the sofa. She stumbles on me and blushes, embarrassed. Her face is close up to mine with barely any distance between us. She pauses and our noses are almost touching as she looks me in the eye. I do not know where to look as she gazes into my eyes before moving away to sit back on the other side of the sofa. I take another gulp to calm my nerves. I am now wondering if Ben was not joking!

BEN IS HAVING lunch with Clare and she is keen to know how he and Sarah are getting along with their travelling plans. Ben goes into waffle mode talking about the plans of where they are going. Clare loves how he expresses himself when describing what they have talked about. She goes doe-eyed over him as he uses his hands and arms to theatrically support his conversation. They both laugh at his comical story.

Clare wants only to lean over and give him a kiss.

JULIE and I are halfway through our lunch and I am feeling tipsy after one and a half glasses. Julie is looking at me differently, which I put down to feeling drunk. We have been talking about our weekends and laughing about new gossip that she has picked up.

When the wine is finished, she grabs something from her handbag. It is a small bottle of vodka. She suggests starting on that next, but that we should drink it from the bottle. I take the first sip and then Julie takes a mouthful. I feel so light-headed in the middle of the afternoon. Julie starts chuckling to herself as she looks at me. A couple of times we lock eyes; I am not sure why she is looking at me differently.

SHE GOES to take the bottle of vodka out of my hands as our faces are an inch apart. She looks my face up and down and then focuses on my lips. My eyes are bleary now and I do not notice her going in for a kiss. I freeze as she passionately locks lips with me and slips her tongue in my mouth. My movement is lethargic because of the alcohol and so my reaction is too slow to pull away.

After she kisses me, she pulls my legs off the end of the sofa. She then pulls my jeans off, taking my underwear with them. I try to pull them up but she commands me to sit there and not move. She is not threatening or forceful. She is the opposite as she gently slides off my jeans so I am naked from the waist down.

She makes me get on my hands and knees with my feet and rear facing the sofa. She sits behind me with her legs on the outside of my legs. She rests her back against the sofa.

I hear her inhale deeply through her nose. Then I feel liquid being poured down the centre of my bum cheeks. As the warm liquid travels down to my vagina, I feel her tongue licking from my vagina all the way up to my back, in between my bum cheeks. I realise she is sipping the Vodka from my body. It feels unexpectedly good. When she is finished sucking on me, I feel one or two fingers going inside me. Being a woman, she knows exactly where I am sensitive and starts to rub her fingers over the crucial spot. It is not long before I have an orgasm. She keeps going until I have multiple spasms. My body stiffens like I am being electrified. My arms collapse and I fall to my elbows. When she is finished, she flips me over and motions me to wriggle away from her so she can get between my legs.

24

HOW WAS IT FOR YOU?

She goes down on me as she pours more vodka on me. I feel the Vodka trickling over my vagina. The feel of her tongue working on my folds gets me going again. I can feel my nipples getting stiff as she brings me off again. My back arches as she focuses on sucking on my clitoris. I can feel myself leaking fluid from my vagina which has never happened with Ben. She is not missing a drop as I hear her tongue squelching and lapping up my pussy juice and vodka, the two fused together.

She flips me over again so I am lying on my stomach. She lifts my hips up so my bum is in the air again. I think she is going to work on my pussy yet again but I feel her tongue going towards my anus. I thought I would flinch and think of crawling away but I don't. It feels weird but nice as I feel the tip of her tongue licking my rim. Before I know it, she puts a finger inside my anus and the next thing, I let out a groan as she fondles something inside and I orgasm once again. My body quivers as she continues to stimulate me. My body collapses on the floor and I have to beg her to stop. My body needs to recover. She finds it amusing as I beg her to stop, but she teases me as she puts her other fingers in my vagina. Both holes are being diddled. I beg her to stop, but at the same time enjoying what she is doing to me. The more I beg, the more she works her magic on both my G Spots. I can hear her moaning in delight as she laps up my throbbing pussy.

When I feel I cannot go any longer, she suddenly pushes my bum so I lie on my stomach. She then turns me over and passionately kisses me. She slips her tongue in my throat as she pushes her lips against mine. She grabs my left breast as she kisses me. She enjoys twisting my nipple gently as she finishes having her way with me.

While we are still kissing, she suddenly decides to get off me and stand up. She stands behind my head where I have to roll my eyes back to see her. She takes her time pulling her jeans down along with her pants. I avoid looking at her vagina and keep my eyes focused on her. She kicks her jeans aside and sits her naked bum on the floor. She motions me to flip back over and she wriggles closer to my face. She then motions me to return the favour. She grabs the back of my head and tugs at my hair. I reluctantly make stabs with my tongue against her clean-shaven folds. I close my eyes and screw my face up as I peck my tongue on her. She takes a stronger hold of my head and pushes me onto her. I have to concentrate on breathing through my nose. As I inhale, I get the pleasant smell of her body odour and it is welcoming. It makes it easier having to go down on her. I am a virgin all over again, not knowing what I am supposed to do. Julie guides me as she murmurs and I use myself to gauge what I think would turn me on. I start sucking on her clitoris how I liked Julie doing it. I use my fingers inside her and see if she is sensitive in the same places as me. She seems to be enjoying my stab in the dark. She starts to get wet and I can see her juices coating my fingers. I do not want to lick my fingers clean and so I put them in her mouth. She sucks my fingers clean and then I go back to working my fingers inside her tight pussy. She feels more wet and before I know it, she cums like thunder and squirts in my eye. I am flabbergasted as she apologises and is sorry for not warning me. After she literally cums on my face, she wants me to clean her soaking pussy with my tongue.

I assume it will taste awful as I run my tongue along the folds of her hairless vagina. I find the taste unoffensive and simply get on with it. She quietly groans as I work on cleaning her up. She leans back, to make sure I can get into every nook and cranny of her undercarriage. She asks me to get deep inside to ensure I do a proper job. So, I use my fingers to part her folds and struggle to get my tongue in there. When I think I am almost done, she only has another orgasm and I have to clean her up again as she squirts more juice. Some of it goes on my rug. I will need to clean that up later before Ben comes home.

When I tell her that she is nice and clean now, she stands up and puts her underwear and her jeans back on. I sit up and rest my back against my sofa in a daze not knowing what exactly happened. When she has finished adjusting herself, she kneels in front of me and kisses me passionately again. When she pulls away, she smiles and tells me that I tasted great and I was good for a beginner. I stare into space and wonder how on earth it went from having a nice lunch to having full-blown oral sex.

Julie says that she will remember this and thought I was not bad. She hopes that I enjoyed her on me. I am too stunned to respond. I am not offended, nor do I feel violated. I am totally in shock over what happened. She finishes packing away the hamper with empty packaging and checks to see if she has left anything. She then lets herself out of my apartment, leaving me to explain to Ben why there is a stain my rug.

BEN IS ready to leave work and head to Sarah's place, so he waits for the lift to arrive on his floor. He is wearing a navy blue slim fit two-piece suit, with black leather loafers. Clare is rushing towards the lift hoping not to miss it and stands next to Ben. She is wearing beige suit trousers and a thin striped blouse with a beige tank top, flat brown shoes and a raincoat. Ben politely smiles at her as he thinks about what he would like to do tonight with Sarah. They have not made any specific plans. He knows that she will be tired from her last day at work. He has noticed that she is getting more fatigued but she is in denial.

While Ben is engrossed in his thoughts, he does not notice Clare looking at him in a sexual way. The lift finally arrives and it is empty. They both walk inside the lift to go down to the ground floor, which is on street level.

While Ben is still deep in thought, Clare cannot help herself pouncing on him. Ben is startled as he did not expect that. He pushes her away but she thrusts herself on him again and tries putting her tongue inside his mouth.

Ben slides away from her and composes himself; 'How can you come on to me after all I have said about Sarah?'

Clare catches her breath and says, 'I can't help the way I feel about you.'

Ben does not see her that way anymore, so he adds, 'I moved on.'

Clare ignores his words. 'How you talk about Sarah turns me on.'

Ben cannot believe how infatuated she is. 'What was wrong with Mark?'

Clare continues pecking at his lips and panting, 'It was not fair leading him on.'

Ben is struggling with her advances. 'If it was another time, I would have. But I am with Sarah.'

Clare still ignores his words, 'Let me feel you inside me. Only this one more time.'

THE LIFT STOPS with a ping and the doors open. Clare quickly pulls away in case there is someone waiting for the lift. They both adjust themselves and Ben is stunned and does not know how to react. His hair is a mess from her pushing her fingers through it.

Ben has to push the button to stop the doors from closing again. Clare is wondering what he is thinking now. He is still dazed and confused as to why Clare pounced on him after him confiding in her for so many days.

As they walk towards the revolving doors, they go to pass the ladies' toilets on the left. Clare takes this opportunity to make a last-ditch attempt. Clare tells him that she needs to use the ladies' bathroom. She grabs him and drags him into the toilet. Ben does not expect it and fails to push himself away from her.

CLARE SHOVES her tongue in his mouth once again, making sure that she makes the most of whatever happens. She assumes that he will reject her but at least she will not have the regret of not trying.

Ben grapples with her arms to try to force her off him while trying to make sure that he does not harm her. Clare starts to feel his crotch to make him aroused and encourage him to go along with her advancements.

After a few moments, Clare is about to give up realising that Ben really does love Sarah and that he has no interest in cheating on her. But she is taken aback when he finally lets her continue pecking him all over his face and mouth. She makes sure that she can get as much sensual excitement before he changes his mind.

Ben cannot imagine him and Sarah having future intimacy due to her condition. He knows that she is going to start getting sick, soon after she heals from her appendix operation. He realises the chemistry is still there and fails to fight the urges.

She pulls away from his mouth to see in his eyes if he is willing to still continue. His eyes give her the go-ahead to get on her knees and pull out his cock.

She smiles at his manhood as she remembers how she last held it and proceeds to give him a blow job.

Ben feels her hot breath cascading over his penis and starts to remember how she was over six months ago. Clare can remember how she used to get him going and applies her technique. She dribbles her saliva over the end of his penis and uses her tongue to swirl the foamy lather. She can see how turned he is getting as his body squirms. She follows his direction working her mouth around his shaft, seeing if it has a positive effect.

She has missed his cock and enjoys having it inside her mouth. She loves the way it tastes and the fact that he is circumcised. Clare does not stop until he has cum. She can feel him starting to have an orgasm as his body stiffens. She pulls away to watch some pre-cum dribble out and then a white substance seep out. She quickly laps at his cum before it he makes a mess on the floor. When she is finished, she stands up and whispers in his ear, asking how he found it. He is too exhausted and breathless to give an answer. She calmly walks out of the bathroom without him. He leaves it a minute to put his cock away and make sure she is not around.

WHEN HE GETS HOME, he cannot quite believe what happened tonight. He walks in through the front door and cannot face Sarah. He feels like he has betrayed her.

I HEAR the door go and I am grateful that Ben is home now. I cannot mention today as he is not going to believe me.

When Ben walks in, I can see he looks stunned and shocked. I panic thinking she has his number and texted him. I ask if he is okay and he says nothing.

We are both sat on the sofa, upright, with similar messy hair and the look of shock. We look like we have put our fingers in an electric socket.

I do not face Ben but I ask how his day was. 'I hope your day was not like mine.'

Ben does not face me. 'I don't know. Did it involve having a close encounter?'

I catch my breath as I am still in shock. 'You won't believe what kind of day I had. Julie really did pull all out the stops.'

Ben murmurs, 'Well, Clare certainly pulled out the stops as a great listener.'

I wonder what he means. 'I am not being funny, but I need a really deep clean.'

Ben finds that amusing as that is what he was thinking, 'Funny you should say that. I also need a deep clean. What is your reason?'

I have to lie, 'Julie made sure I thoroughly enjoyed her dessert selections. We took turns tasting each other's pudding. How about you?'

Ben looks puzzled, 'That sounds like a lot of dessert. Did it include cream pie? Hope you did not overindulge on dessert.'

I slouch my back into the sofa and think back, 'It was not cream pie, more like warm apple pie. With a little cream.'

Ben slouches his back into the sofa and sighs, 'Well, I didn't exactly have a dessert. Clare thought I needed a massage.'

I wonder why he needed a massage. 'Did you have knots in your muscle?'

Ben's eyebrows raise, 'You could say she stretched out my muscle, to the point where my muscle was stiff.'

I raise my eyebrows and say, 'Hope she did not strain your muscles too hard. Sometimes it can be easy to overstrain.'

Ben catches his breath again. 'Oh, she made sure I did not overstrain.'

We eventually stand up and walk like zombies to the bathroom and both get in the shower together. Ben asks me to spend extra time making sure I clean his manhood thoroughly. I ask him to make sure he cleans my under-carriage thoroughly as well.

Then we end up falling silent and simply go to bed, still stunned by our days.

25

PREPARATIONS

It is now the beginning of April. I have my ninth appointment today. Ben takes time off work to come with me to the hospital. We go straight to the CT Scan room in the purple zone of the hospital. My fifth scan feels quicker compared to the first time.

After the scan, we have to go to see the doctor and sit outside his office, waiting for the results.

WE WAIT for about half an hour before the doctor calls us in to discuss how much further my tumour has developed.

I ask Ben why I have been having these scans. It does not change the outcome. I wonder if Doctor Chopra is hoping for a miracle change or that it proves to be operable.

For a brief moment, I do not even consider what Ben is going through. I have not once asked how he is feeling. We have only talked about accepting this and squeezing in as much activity while I can.

I will discuss this with him later. We are finally asked to come into his office

DOCTOR CHOPRA TELLS us to sit down and waits until we are comfortable. Ben holds my hand as we wait for him to tell us what we already know. I do not know why I agreed to have fortnightly scans. They benefit the doctor more than me.

Doctor Chopra examines my scan but he does not show me the film this time. Ben and I briefly glance at each other and break into a slight smile.

Doctor Chopra focuses his eyes on what he can see. 'When I told you that I wanted to monitor you, you were probably thinking what's the point? I have already given you my prediction.'

I wonder why he is telling me what I already know.

Doctor Chopra continues, 'I was hoping that the tumour would continue to grow slowly, thereby giving you hope of extending your life beyond six months so you could have more time to make the most of what you have left.'

Ben has a question straight away. 'We are looking at going travelling soon. We were going to tell you today. Get back before Sarah gets too sick.'

Doctor Chopra's face says it all. 'Your tumour was growing at a rate of two millimetres per month. Your tumour was still the size of a pea, but it has almost doubled in size. Based on this, your life expectancy will be considerably shorter.'

Ben starts to well up as he asks, 'How much time?'

My emotions take over and I begin to tear up unexpectedly, 'Just give it to us.'

Doctor Chopra is about to tell us but has to take a moment; 'We are looking at two months.'

I almost fall off my chair and am overwhelmed with emotions of shock for myself and sadness for Ben. Ben holds me to prevent me from falling. No matter how you anticipate the answer, it still does not prepare you.

Doctor Chopra continues, 'I suggest you hold off travelling. In the next month, you will start to feel the effects that I told you about when you were first told about your tumour.'

Ben wants to be reminded of those effects, so he asks 'What are they, again?'

Doctor Chopra reminds me about my temporal lobe; 'Based on where yours is, you will eventually start to experience short-term memory loss, difficulty with hearing and speaking. Your hallucinations will get worse; you might even start hearing voices. As the tumour reduces space inside your skull, you will begin to suffer dizziness and headaches. You will experience nosebleeds because your body will be trying to relieve pressure.'

Eventually, my mind switches off as he continues, like he is white noise in the background. I start to makes new plans for myself.

IN THE CAR during the drive back to my place, I cannot stop thinking about my life expectancy going from six months to two months. I assumed he would give me a year.

There is silence in the car as we do not say a word to each other. I assume that Ben is thinking how much time he has left with me.

When we get home, we feel mentally drained and sit down in the living room. After what seems ages, Ben finally admits that travelling is out of the window. I slowly nod my head in agreement.

I ask Ben if he still wants to be around. He is surprised that I asked and is upset by my question. He makes it clear that he does not want to end our relationship. We sit there in comfortable silence. We are still numb from the appointment.

A FEW DAYS HAVE PASSED. My parents handled the news very badly, unsurprisingly. We cried uncontrollably together. Ben looked on, letting the three of us have our moment. He made us hot drinks and was there for moral support. With all that has been going on, I have not had a chance to tell my best friends.

For some reason, Julie comes into my thoughts. I wonder what happened that day. One minute we were having lunch and getting tipsy; the next minute she makes a pass at me. Thinking back, I now know she had planned it. The times she would glare at me, in faculty meetings. I used to think she hated me for no apparent reason. I guess she wanted to know what I was like before it was too late for her to satisfy her curiosity.

I recall how I experienced it. At first, it felt uncomfortable watching a woman perform on me when my whole life was focused on being with a man. But when I was not able to see what she was doing it could have easily been a man. But the difference is that her tongue was very feminine compared to Ben's. That was the difference and the fact that I did not have to give her hints. She certainly knew where to push my buttons. I can understand why a woman would be happy to be a lesbian. I think of Georgina and have an idea how she can enjoy a same-sex relationship.

Thinking of Julie and our sexual experience, while sipping coffee on my sofa, helps me not to think about my current situation.

I wonder if I could be a lesbian because it felt surprisingly good having her mouth and fingers work on me. My sexual orientation has not changed at all, so could I be bi-sexual? My feelings for Ben and our intimacy have not changed at all.

We have been having more sex since finding out. I do not know if I am merely trying to squeeze in as much experience as possible.

I find it strange that if I was not sick, she would not have made a pass at me. I would never have experienced it. If I was a man, it would never have happened.

I FEEL the urge to play dance music. I am bored and want to change my mood. As I start feeling the music and naturally dance to the rhythm, I start to think of my imaginary friends and wish they were here now.

I put on music from my teenage days and close my eyes so I can enjoy the music more. I stomp my feet, flinging my arms in the air and spinning around to the music.

When I eventually open my eyes, I see my five squirrels, the gnome and my recent new friend, Paul. They are standing in front of me. They put a smile on my face and they begin to dance to the music. We stand next to each other, side by side. Then, in unison, we dance to our left and right, spinning around part way.

We are having a real laugh and again, it takes my mind off what is happening in life. We get into a circle and each, in turn, go into the centre and show off our own dance moves. The rest of us clap and praise their movements.

We go on for a good half an hour. The music reaches the end and we all crash to the floor. We are on our backs as we giggle amongst ourselves. After I catch my breath, I sit up and they are no longer with me.

I decide that I want to think about making a will and I want Ben to help me make it. I already have an idea what I want to write.

I GO into the spare bedroom to the box that I used to clear my office. I find a pad of paper and a pen. I go back into the living room and start listing out my instructions.

While I am listing what I want in the will, I text my friends Natalie, Georgina, Kerry and Mercedes to arrange a meeting for the first time in ages. I want to meet up with them in the day time and think a Sunday will be good. I also text them to ask how each of them are with their lives.

Natalie has no issues and life is good for her family. I assumed that would be the response I would get. Georgina is still struggling to have a baby. I already knew before I received her text. She also says that there are a few things they have to forego for their wedding. I ask them what they are having to give up. I feel guilty as I am now financially secure. It makes me cry a little because that is no different to finding out that I will never have children.

Kerry is content, as per usual, and she has no problems in her life. She keeps herself busy as usual. She has always been an inspiration to me as I see her as a free spirit. I felt more drawn to her and before she met her partner, we had been as thick as thieves since junior school. We did everything together. When I went for my walks earlier in the week, it was taking walks where Kerry and I went. I realise that she was my childhood life. When she met her partner, I felt jealous and I do not know why. Even to this day, I have no idea why I felt threatened by her partner. She would never say but he never really liked me and I know it is not in my head when he gives me daggers. I think he fancies me - why else would he be funny around me? He has never made a pass at me but I can only assume that must be it. There have been two people hating each other as friends and then, out of nowhere, end up fancying each other. I think out of my four friends, Kerry will be the one I will miss the most.

Mercedes is content with her life and has recently bought a dog to keep her company. I feel for her, like Georgina not being able to have kids. I know that she lies to herself about how much she would love to have a baby. I have asked why they do not find a surrogate mother. The idea does not float her boat. I ask if she would be a surrogate mother if someone asked her. She finds my question thought-provoking.

By the time I am finished texting back and forth to my friends, I think I have finished my will. I wonder whether to go into London now or give it to Ben tonight, so he can legalise it tomorrow. I text him about it and he thinks it will be nice to go for dinner tonight in London on the spur of the moment, so I set out to travel into London and go to his office.

IT IS after two o'clock and I should be at his office by four. I leave now and walk over to the train station. It only takes fifteen minutes to get there.

When I eventually get on the train, the L.E.D sign on the ceiling of the train shows that it will take an hour and twenty minutes to get into Euston.

While on the train, the conversation with my friends via text makes me think. I think about the future of my friends and feel sad that I will not see their future unfold. I will never find out if Georgina and her fiancée, Freiya, finally get a chance to have a baby.

As yet, I have not mentioned to Ben about an idea that I have been thinking about in the past week. I found out that I can afford to pay for both of us on a trip. It will cost £350,000 between us to fly sixty-two miles above Earth to what is called a 'Karman Line'. It is the line which separates Earth's atmosphere and outer space. Now our world travel is not going ahead, I at least want to achieve this before it is too late. I have till sometime in June. I want to go before the end of May.

THE JOURNEY from Euston to his office did not feel that long. His office is walking distance from Waterloo station.

I use my mobile phone app to get to his building. It is strange going to his place of work when I have never seen it before. I pictured him working in a stuffy cramped office in a Victorian building.

When I get to his work, I notice it is a modern building covered with glass panels, so you can see inside. The interior of the reception is light and airy with contemporary furniture against white walls and white marble floors.

As I approach the building from across the road, I see Ben with a girl and they are laughing together. She has her arm through his as they walk in through the revolving door. I assume this must be Clare. He seems a lot happier being in her company. I do not remember us being like that before my appendix operation.

I keep back to continue to observe their behaviour together. I feel myself getting jealous that she is able to put a smile on his face easily. After they walk to the lift and get inside, I walk in and go to reception.

I TELL reception that I have arranged to see a solicitor, calling my boyfriend by his full name, Benjamin Chandler. I do not want to give her the perception that he is my boyfriend in case Ben thinks it is unprofessional. The man behind reception asks me to take a seat and he will bring him down.

I notice the chairs are orange and slightly puffed up. They feel comfortable and I have a view of the outside world to keep me distracted. I wish I had a book with me to keep me company.

After a while, Ben comes to greet me and is pleased to see me. He gives me a hug and kisses me passionately. It surprises me, as I assumed he would keep it professional. We do not hold hands but we stand close together.

He asks me what I am thinking of including in the will. He states the obvious of making sure I include my parents and any other immediate family first. Then if there are any friends, leave them to last. He tells me that, because of ethical reasons and the fact that we are in a relationship, he cannot be involved in the discussions. I understand where he is coming from and ask who will be helping me to draw it up.

Ben says that it will be one of his colleagues that he trusts to ensure my will does not leave any loose ends.

I do mention that I saw him cosying up with another girl. I leave it for a more appropriate time.

AFTER WE REACH HIS FLOOR, we go into his office first. His mannerism is different when at work. He is very conservative and professional, completely the opposite to when he is at home. I find it strange. I try to have a playful conversation with him like how we talk at home, but he struggles to adjust. We end up talking about why I have come to the sudden decision to get a will drawn up. I miss the part out where I saw my friends again. He then asks why the sudden hurry to come over today to arrange one. I tell him that I simply felt the need to get it done now, instead of wasting a day. I thought he would understand but he tells me that he would have taken my notes in tomorrow. I know he would have but I also wanted to see what his office was like and see him. But I do not tell him that part.

We make small talk about where to go for dinner in London. Someone knocks on Ben's door and interrupts our conversation. It is the colleague who is going to write up my will.

Ben is abrupt and says that he will see me after I finish talking with his colleague.

HIS COLLEAGUE IS TALL, slim and balding on top, with red hair which going grey. He is wearing a pair of round-rimmed glasses. His three-piece suit is light brown with a tartan chequered style pattern blue shirt.

He walks us into a conference room and makes us both a coffee from a posh machine.

The room seems overkill for a simple meeting. He asks for my list which I have crumpled in my pocket. He asks what I have in my estate and the only thing I can think of is my three million pounds. He splutters his coffee when I tell him this. He smiles, embarrassed, and checks to see if he spilt any on his suit.

He starts again and asks, apart from the money, what I have in my estate. I tell him that it is simple as I do not own my apartment and do not have anything else in my name. He finds my case simple and easy to arrange. He asks who I want mentioned in the will and that's when it gets complicated. I tell him that I have a couple of really close friends as well as my parents. It is also technical. When I tell him what I have planned, his eyes light up and he makes a long whistling sound.

CLARE WALKS into Ben's office asking why Sarah has come in. He is cryptic with her and changes the subject, discussing her case. Clare takes the hint and asks for his advice on a menial technical article. Ben welcomes the distraction and asks her to sit down.

Deep down, he was caught off guard by Sarah wanting to get a will written out of the blue. It makes it even more real that she is slowly slipping away from his fingers. He wants to make the most of being with her on the trip. He does not want to deal with the rough road ahead, such as discussing what she will be leaving behind. He is not ready to start letting her go.

AFTER AN HOUR of going through the ins and outs of my will; he tells me that he can have it drawn up in a few days, considering my situation. I can get my affairs in order. When we are finished, I go back to Ben's office after asking someone for directions.

26

LIFE MOVES ON

I see the same woman in Ben's office and it stops me in my tracks. I watch them through the glass wall. They have not noticed me.

She is giggling and touching his forearm. He seems to be relaxed by her touchy-feely ways. I picture them getting together when I am gone. Getting together sometime in the not so distant future. I feel jealous that she could provide a lifetime partner, marriage and... children. I sense something happened between them before I came on the scene. The way they are behaving tells me that they are not just friends; they must have had a history for them to be as close as that. Knowing that he is in a relationship, Ben should feel uncomfortable. I assume this is the woman he told me about, his ex-girlfriend.

I have an epiphany. Out of nowhere, my perception of us changes. I can no longer see him being with me to the end. I can no longer see us being a couple. I see myself being alone when I am on my deathbed. I feel I have lost him already, and I am only realising this now.

I am scared that if he is with me any longer, this girl will find someone else and he will miss his boat. It will be my fault that I did not let him go sooner. I could not live with myself if I stop him from finding another meaningful relationship. I can see her taking care of him after I have gone, not that I want to think that he will mourn for me for months.

I have decided to let him go now. I will tell him over dinner tonight. It will hurt me more than it will him. I will not be around to see him marry, have children and have a fulfilling life.

· · ·

I WALK into his office unannounced, pretending that I have not noticed her in his office. Ben appears startled and moves away from her. I act like I am not jealous at all and wait for Ben to introduce his work colleague.

He surprises me when I find out it is Clare. Wow, I did not realise how attractive she was. He did forget to mention that and I can tell that she likes him. I wonder if anything has happened in the past.

Clare smiles at me without feeling awkward and so I assume she does not know that I am his girlfriend. She would not feel relaxed if she knew about my current condition and us being partners.

I cannot help but be envious of Clare's attractiveness and the fact she has her whole life in front of her to make things work with Ben.

I do my best to hide my jealousy, 'Nice to meet you. Ben has mentioned you a couple of times.'

Clare smiles and shows surprise, 'Oh, I didn't know that. I'm surprised my ears were not burning.'

I laugh with her as I ask, 'Ben, when do you want to go for dinner?'

Ben is awkward; 'We can go in the next five minutes. Clare, I will see you later.'

Clare suddenly realises that she needs to leave us alone and walks out of his office. I mention to him my observation regarding Clare's behaviour. Ben shrugs off Clare's behaviour as being friendly. Nothing more is said.

WE FIND A PIZZA RESTAURANT NEARBY. We have already ordered and are drinking our alcohol as we wait. I ordered a medium red glass of wine and Ben ordered a bottle of premium beer. While waiting for our main course, I have to do something that I will regret but need to do.

I think this is a good place as we are in a social environment, so I say, 'I am letting you go, Ben.'

Ben is stunned, 'Why? I love you. I want to be with you to the end. There is nothing else in my life.'

I can see how his life is going to be laid out. 'Yes, you do. You have Clare. If I do not let you go now, you will lose her.'

Ben does not agree; 'Why do you think Clare is suited to me? That we would ever get together? We are work colleagues and good friends. The thought of it is weird.'

I still believe Clare is suitable for him, so I go on, 'I can see you getting married to her.'

Ben ignores my comment. 'How long have you been thinking this?'

I am honest with him; 'When I saw you two in your office. It has only just dawned on me. It never crossed my mind until then. Promise me you will give it a go. I know she will not wait for you. She is intelligent, pretty. It won't take her that long to find some else to go out with.'

Ben might be coming round to the idea, 'You have been thinking about this a lot.'

I TELL him how my circumstances have made me see things clearly. 'When you are told you have not long to live, your outlook on life changes overnight. I quickly realise what is more important; you. I already know how my life is going to be.'

Ben is staring into his pizza; 'This is the first time we have talked about this. It takes dumping me to open up.'

I see his point. 'I guess I needed time to digest everything and arrange my thoughts.'

Ben has something on his mind, so he goes on, 'I have something to confess.'

I am alarmed about what it could be, 'What is that?'

Ben pauses before he confesses; 'That day when I came over to your place. We both had a shower together.'

I have to think for a moment, 'Ah, yes. That was the last time we had a shower together. What about it?'

Ben holds his fork up and twirls it on his pizza, 'Clare made a pass at me and... gave me a blow job. There, I said it.'

I am open-mouthed but definitely not sad. 'Wow. I knew it! I knew there was something going on between you two. I assume you had something before that because a woman doesn't do that without taking a risk.'

Ben confirms, 'We split up because I was focusing on my uncle's illness. I didn't tell her that we were an item. I keep my private life private from work. It was my fault. She would never have done that if she knew about you.'

I do not tell him about Julie as I do not think it is relevant. We end up talking about gossip on social media and television, making each other laugh. We are finding it easy to become friends.

WE WALK BACK SLOWLY, not saying anything. I make the most of what little time I have left with Ben. We go back to Ben's office because he left his briefcase behind. As we go to walk through the revolving doors, Clare is just leaving herself. I wonder if God is playing a part in this.

We walk towards her and I go up to her and say, 'I want you to find happiness with him. Don't tiptoe about. One thing I have learnt is that life is not guaranteed. If you have an opportunity to do something, don't let it go by.'

Clare stares at me oddly and then turns to Ben. Ben tells Clare that he will explain later. I leave them together and go home by myself.

. . .

AFTER AN HOUR and twenty minutes of train travel, I finally reach Milton Keynes Central Station. I walk back to my place, get into the car and drive to my parents' house. When I knock on my parents' door, Mum answers and I instantly break down in tears. Mum grabs me and walks me indoors. She listens and doesn't judge.

A FEW DAYS have passed and it is now Saturday. Ben came round yesterday to collect his few things. He left the map of our trip we were going to do in a week's time.

It is lunchtime and I have heated a tin of chicken soup, which I am eating in the living room. I feel a little sorry for myself as I do not have a boyfriend anymore and I am not seeing my friends until five o'clock. I went for a run this morning, thinking that it would help to take my mind off Ben, but it made me think of him even more and I thought running faster would make him leave my thoughts.

When I was in the shower, I started questioning if I made the right decision and part of me wanted to run over to his house to say I made a mistake. However, when Ben came yesterday to collect his things, he told me that he was listening to my advice with Clare.

Spending time alone has really cleared my head as I now know what I want to do with the remaining time I have left.

By the time I finish eating and getting food shopping done, it is time to go round to Georgina's house. Everyone is going to be there.

I DRIVE to Woburn to get to her house and make sure I am about twenty minutes late, so I know everyone will be there. I don't want to be standing around and getting anxious. I want to come and say it, then get on with the rest of the night.

WHEN I GET to her house, I ring the doorbell and wait for one of the girls to answer. I start to get nervous over having to announce it. It still has not sunk in as I feel totally fine; I have no symptoms or pain. If it was not for the hallucinations, I would be none the wiser.

After a few minutes, Freiya, Georgina's soon-to-be-wife answers the door. She has a glass of wine in her hand and is tipsy.

I FOLLOW her through the hallway to the back of the house into an open-plan living room. Two of them are on the floor or bean bags and the other two are on the sofa. I have nowhere to sit down. I thought this was going to be easy but all five pairs of eyes are on me now, including Freiya.

Kerry is the first to ask what the big news was. I giggle nervously, wishing that I had not arranged this. They make room for me to sit on the sofa. When I am settled in and everyone is comfortable, they wait for me to start.

I swallow to allow myself time to gather my thoughts. Mercedes prompts me by shouting 'boyfriend' and everyone cheers. I wish I could have ended it with Ben next week now. I smile, embarrassed at not being ready to tell them. Kerry moves over and coaxes me out of my shell.

I eventually tell them; 'A couple of things have come up which mean I have to be honest with you guys. I didn't want you to think that I was ignoring you and question why I never made it to your events. A classic example is Georgina's wedding.'

There is silence with puzzled faces and Georgina naturally asks, 'Why can't you come? I want you to be a bridesmaid. You can't not come to the wedding.'

I begin to well up, 'Because I physically will not be here.'

Natalie half laughs and naturally questions my comment, 'What do you mean? You will be abroad somewhere?'

I smile and chuckle to myself, 'That is one way of putting it.'

Mercedes sees sadness behind my eyes as a tear rolls down my cheek. 'Come on, you can tell us. You are worrying us'

Kerry goes to hold my hand, 'It's okay. You are amongst friends.'

I finally tell them the long-winded version; 'Back in late January, I had an inflamed appendix that eventually burst. I was rushed into hospital.'

Georgina interrupts, 'But you're fine now, right? You look okay.'

I try to explain subtly, 'After my surgery... this is embarrassing. A nurse caught me talking to myself. I mean talking to some friends that I started hallucinating back in November last year. That lead to being seen by a specialist.'

Kerry sees me struggling to continue, and reassures me, 'It is okay. We are your best friends.'

I take a few short breaths and continue; 'His name is Doctor Chopra. He told me that I have this mass in my brain. In the temporal lobe. Somewhere near the base of the neck.'

Georgina is optimistic, 'Yeah, but they are going to take it out, right? So, is that why you won't make my wedding? You're having the operation and recovery around that time?'

My four best friends and Freiya slowly stop being upbeat and smiling when I tell them, 'It is inoperable. I have been given a time frame.'

Kerry begins to tear up which does not help me put on a brave face, 'How long, Sarah?'

I fight hard to hold back the tears. 'Two months. Was six months. But that would have been a push.'

All five girls rush over and huddle with me and cry. It is a while before everyone calms their nerves and gets through the shock.

Eventually, Kerry cannot take it anymore and rushes out of the room. I gently tell everyone that I need to go after her and see she is alright.

I NOTICE the door is wide open and panic about where she could have gone. I quickly rush outside and search for her. I see her standing on the pavement alone, in the distance, in floods of tears. I run after her and catch her before she kneels on the concrete.

I comfort her, 'It's okay. Let it out. I am here.'

Kerry yells out a scream as she cries, 'Not you! Of all people, not you!'

I stay calm and I feel for her as I went through this with my parents and Ben. 'It's okay. Let it out. I am here.'

Kerry is angry at herself; 'It should be me comforting you, not the other way round.'

I jokingly agree with her, 'Yeah, you should be.'

Kerry turns to bargaining; 'Can't you just make it go away, somehow? I wanted to see you fall in love, get married, have our kids hang out. Of all people, you deserve to have that.'

I have already been through the bargaining stage, 'That's life. And one day, you will be dying. It is the tapestry of life. There is no rhyme or reason. And for now, it is my time. But it is okay. I will just be in another place. I will have a cup of tea waiting for you. But for now, I am here now. And that is what is more important. I want to spend my last remaining days with my best friends. Especially you. I hope your husband does not want to beat me up.'

Kerry begins to laugh. 'I will deal with him. You have always been in my life.'

I have something I need to ask her. 'There is something that I want you to help me do. It is all booked up. Did it the next day when I found out how long I have to live. I don't want to talk about it but in a month's time, I want you to come with me somewhere. I will explain in more detail nearer the time.'

Kerry does not hesitate, I expect because she is my closest friend; 'Just name it. I will drop anything for you.'

When Kerry cleans up her mascara, we head back to the house.

WHEN WE GET BACK to the house, Georgina and Freiya have already agreed to move their wedding to the beginning of May. My five friends talk about changing the date of the venue and church, using me as the reason, then discussing the catering and decorations, explaining that it is not a problem as they cannot afford a lot. I think of my lottery win and ask Georgina in private what her ideal wedding would be. I mentally take note of what she would love to have and I put it into my mobile so I do not forget.

I will make sure she gets what she wants and not only what she needs. I will pay for everything she cannot afford. That will be my wedding present to her. It is not like I will have the time to spend it all by myself.

I cannot believe that I will be able to see Georgina and Freiya get married before my time is up. I will have a memory to take with me.

I mention very briefly that I went out with Ben and, in private, that he was my first.

27

TURN OF EVENTS

It is the week before Georgina and Freiya's wedding. The last three weeks have flown by, which scares me, as I am heading closer to the unknown.

Since splitting up with Ben, I have been able to spend a lot more time with my parents without the stress of alternating. I have also seen my best friends virtually every week, helping with the wedding plans. I have secretly taken care of all of the wish list. I do not know how I have managed to keep quiet about the car to pick them up separately from their respective parents' homes, their honeymoon, upgrading the menu at the reception and paying for Freiya's relatives to fly over. It has helped by giving me a huge distraction.

For a couple of days, I have been feeling slight headaches but they are infrequent. I have had a couple of nosebleeds but put it down to needing to slow down. Luckily, they have happened when I have been home alone. I do not want to get embarrassed in front of anyone.

My hallucinations have become more frequent as well and my friends showed their sympathy for my split from Ben. They have kept me company while organising the wedding.

Tonight is Georgina and Freiya's hen do at the same place I met Ben. The girls remember but they want to have lasting memories of the five of us. I do not want them to forget me.

Kerry has the cash and tells everyone that she is putting money behind the bar as a wedding gift, hiding the fact that I am the one who is paying for the whole night out. I can see in Kerry's face that she feels she is betraying everyone, but I reassure her that it is okay and that I have put in place a plan for everyone to find out later.

. . .

I SUDDENLY FEEL like dancing and wander off onto the dance floor. I feel my personality is changing as I am confident dancing by myself. I slowly start hallucinating again and see my friends one by one. They want to dance with me and so we stand side by side and wait for the next track to kick in. The song is by Georgina and is called 'About Work The Dance Floor'; how appropriate. We start to dance like we did in my apartment on the same day I broke up with Ben. We slide to the right, spin round and slide to the right. Then we crouch down and slowly stand up as we twist our bodies. We are really getting into the rhythm.

I notice that the people around us are making space for us, so we can show them how it is done. I glance up and see my hen do party across the way near the bar. They cannot believe that I am taking over the floor. People are now circulating me and clapping as I continue to rock my moves, as I dance with my imaginary friends.

The music changes and the next track is a golden oldy called 'Saturday Night' by 'Whigfield'; appropriate considering it is Saturday night. This is another great tune and we all join in the routine for the song. If heaven is like this, I will be happy.

I recite how the dance move goes and then begin with my friends. We clap our hands in the air and move our arms to the right and left in a wave-like motion. We then put our left leg forward and with our arms pointing upwards. Then rest our right elbow on the palm of our left palm and move our right arm round and round. We repeat the same move with our right leg forward and our left elbow in our right palm. With both forearms horizontal, roll our forearms around each other with our bums stuck out.

The squirrels are cute with their tails poking out from their bums.

We then repeat the last move but thrust our hips forward. We slightly flex our knees and put our right hand above our right knee, then our left hand above our left knee. Then we put our right hand on our right buttock and our left hand on our left buttock.

The squirrels are adorable as they put their hands on either side of their tails. Really cute bums.

With our hands still on our bums, we jump forward and back, jump a quarter of a turn clockwise, clap our hands high and then repeat the moves all over again.

BEFORE I KNOW IT, the people around us begin to join in as we go to repeat the dance routine again. I am in my element. This is the closest thing to heaven. The five squirrels are really getting into it, second time around.

The gnome is beaming with delight at having one of our last times together. Paul talks above the noise to tell me that if he was real, he would go out with me. I think that is sweet and I tell him that I would like that too.

Georgina's friends are still observing at us, open-mouthed, not quite believing what they are seeing. The song finally finishes and all of us cheer and hug each other. I get lost amongst the crowd and try to see where my friends are, but they have disappeared. I quickly check to make sure that no one is staring at me or noticed that I had one of my hallucinations. I then go back to my party and they grab me and cannot believe that I had that in me. They keep saying that I commanded the floor and made everyone else dance with me. I simply shrug it off.

For a moment, I have a slight wobble and put it down to spinning around on the dance floor. Kerry grabs hold of me to check I am okay. I have never seen her so protective over me and I nod my head and blame it on the alcohol, which I have not touched. Kerry is very caring towards me and our eyes meet and we catch ourselves gazing into each other's eyes. For a moment, I think she is going to make a pass at me like Julie did. But I am only being ridiculous.

I find her attentiveness towards me quite sweet.

The rest of the night involved drinking games and the girls made sure I was not involved in the alcohol because of my condition. They bought me virgin drinks but still included me in the games. They were very kind, taking care of me like one of their baby sisters.

WHEN THE NIGHT FINISHES, they do not mess around and ensure that I get home first and even walk me to my front door. For some reason, Kerry wants to let them go ahead and feel she wants to say something to me. She goes to speak but hesitates. She cannot get the words out and gives me a huge hug. She does not want to let go. I can smell her hair and the perfume on her skin. I do not want her to go now and want to ask her to come in for a nightcap. But she suddenly lets go and kisses me on the cheek and promises that she will call me before the day of the wedding.

THE FOLLOWING WEEK, I am getting back to finalising things for the wedding. I split my week between home and my parents' house.

My parents knew not to smother me but I can see in their eyes that if they could, they would, without hesitation. Each hug they give me is longer and harder and they try not to show their emotions. They do not want to waste what time they have with me on shedding tears.

At my parents' house, I enjoy making phone calls and payments for the wedding. They can see how happy I am and how well my life is. There is the odd occasion when I get a nosebleed and do not realise, so they patiently let me know without freaking out. I behave like it is nothing so I do not worry them. I have not told them why they occur as I do not want them to be reminded that I am closer to my end day.

IT IS THE BIG DAY. I travel in the car I organised for Georgina. I laid on a Bentley Ghost for each of the girls. We will meet Freiya at the church, but they have arranged for Georgina to be at the altar first.

While travelling to the church, I feel another headache coming on and try to block it out. It is a faint dull pain and so it is bearable.

There is one other bridesmaid who I met at the hen do and the three of us have a jokey conversation, laughing at each other's comments. We tease Georgina about whether or not Freiya will turn up.

WHEN WE ARRIVE at the church, the driver parks outside the gate. The other bridesmaid and myself help her get out and adjust her dress. Then we walk behind her as the three of us go inside. Everyone seems to be here already as it is very full. There is not one person who is missing. I find myself smiling at the guests on both sides.

When we reach the place where the vicar is standing, we have to stand to the left. Now we are just waiting for Freiya to arrive.

My head starts to slowly hurt more, like someone is tightening a vice around my head. I tell myself that it is only another half an hour. I only have to bear with this for another half an hour, then I can go somewhere quiet to ride it out.

EVENTUALLY, Freiya starts walking down the aisle but we bridesmaids cannot see through the congregation, as they are on their feet now.

I feel myself starting to feel faint and continue to tell myself to keep it together.

I can finally see Freiya as she stands next to Georgina. I welcome the distraction as they prepare to make their vows. I feel my nose getting runny like I have a cold. I am praying that it is not another nosebleed.

FINALLY, the vicar is declaring that they are now married and I can hopefully slope off and clear my nose. Also, I need to find a shop to get some headache tablets.

The vicar announces that they can now kiss and everyone shouts encouragement to them. As Georgina and Freiya start to kiss, I feel myself collapsing and touch my nose to see blood on my finger. My legs start to struggle to hold me up. I try to mentally will my body not to fall down. I feel my legs starting to give way and I collapse on the ground. I still have my wits about me, but I am struggling to stay conscious. I feel stupid and try to quickly stand up thinking that no one has noticed. I hear the other bridesmaids gasping and a few minutes later, I hear Kerry's voice. I start to get embarrassed and flustered, thinking that I have ruined Georgina's wedding day.

I hear Kerry's voice, 'Sarah, are you okay? Someone, call the ambulance. Call the ambulance!'

I put on a brave face and say, 'I'm fine. I felt light-headed. I just need a moment. I can't ruin the wedding. Kerry, can you get me a tissue and help clean me up? I cannot ruin this wedding.'

Kerry ignores me and asks the other bridesmaids to give me room. I see Georgina coming over and I brace myself for a barrage of offence.

I quickly try to apologise as I fight the tears; 'I am so sorry. Please forgive me. I did not mean for this to happen.'

Georgina pulls my hair away from my bloody nose and then strokes my face, 'No, to have you here, to see you, don't you get it? My day is complete. I thought you would not make it.'

I am still crying. 'But I did not give you a chance to kiss the bride.'

Freiya makes a joke of it, 'You saved me from a fate worse than death. You know how much of a bad kisser she is.'

Georgina goes along with it and adds, 'She is right. I was hoping you would faint. You did me a favour.'

The three of us laugh but the pounding inside my head is getting unbearable.

Kerry does not join in our sense of humour, 'Quick. We will drive her there. Georgina, take care of your guests.'

Freiya glances at Georgina and they both say, 'We are going with you. You are not dying on my watch. Come, Georgina, help us get Sarah up.'

I cannot stay conscious as the pressure in my brain makes me pass out.

I WAKE up in hospital thinking that I have been here for days and have missed the reception party. It startles me. I notice Georgina, Freiya, Kerry and her husband Mark. A different doctor comes into the ward. She pulls the curtains so we have privacy from the other patients.

She is a woman about the same age as me with shoulder-length brown hair. 'You gave your friends quite a fright.'

I feel stupid and say, 'I just passed out. It was nothing serious. I am fine now.'

The doctor ignores my comment. 'I am fully aware of your condition. Spoke to your doctor. We have given you a heavy painkiller. Similar to morphine. That is why you can't feel any pain. We did a further scan, as your doctor was worried. Sarah, do you have any family?'

I wish I could see my friends behind the curtain for reassurance. 'Why would I need to see family?'

The doctor is trying to be as delicate as possible; 'Since we last saw you, your tumour has doubled in size. To put it into context, it is now the size of a peach, which is why you ended up collapsing. There is now pressure forming inside. Do you follow me?'

I know what she is saying. 'There is not enough room anymore for the tumour to exist.'

The doctor gently nods at me, 'I am concerned, Sarah. You need looking after now. You cannot continue as you were.'

I need to know if my time frame has reduced, so I ask her, 'How much time do I have left? Tell me straight. Don't sugar-coat it.'

The doctor sighs and sits on my bed. 'If your tumour had behaved itself and grown at the same pace, I would have given you another three or four months.'

I am anxious for her opinion, so I push her; 'A month, two months?'

The doctor catches me short, 'Less than a month. Maybe three weeks at a push.'

My heart sinks and I start to tear up, 'I need to leave. I cannot stay here. I have a wedding to finish.'

The doctor stops me. 'The best thing you can do is take it easy. Let them get back to the wedding. You rest here for a few more hours. You're ill, Sarah. You are going to get worse.'

I have already made my mind up to do one more thing before it is too late. I ask for her to let my friends back in and she pulls the curtain. She leaves me alone and says she will be back in half an hour.

My friends can see that I have been crying again and frantically demand to know what is happening. Kerry holds my hand and I can see her husband giving me daggers. I ignore him and focus on Kerry.

I need Kerry to do one last thing for me and that is it; 'Kerry. Can you go to my flat? There, you will see a dark blue suitcase in the hallway. On top of that suitcase are two flight tickets. Can you pack a few days of clothes and bring those things back here?'

Kerry knows what I am saying and has prepared herself for this, 'Of course. I will be back as soon as possible. Just don't do anything, or I will kill myself and go after you.'

I smile at her, 'It is time now.'

Kerry starts to get emotional. 'Shut up. Please shut up, before I start to cry.'

I go quiet and turn to Georgina and Freiya; 'Again, I am so sorry for ruining your wedding.'

Georgina sits on the side of my bed and, in a quiet voice, she insists, 'You made our day making it to our wedding. That is the best wedding present we could have hoped for.'

I cannot hold it any longer; 'I have paid for you two to go on a honeymoon. I know you could not afford it. I came into some money, so I paid for the things that were on your wish list.'

THEY ARE both in shock and both hug me to say thank you. I wanted to let them know as I would be upset if they did not find out before I died. They then allow Kerry's partner Mark to see me.

MARK STANDS a few feet away from me. I motion him to come closer. I need to make peace before I leave.

I stare him in the eye and say, 'I know you have never liked me from day one. It is why I stopped coming over. What did I ever do to upset you?'

Mark is taken aback as he does not expect my attitude, 'I never hated you. Not really.'

I roll my eyes and ask the same question again, 'I have upset you. I will not see you after today. I want closure, Mark.'

Mark does not know how to begin, 'All Kerry has done to this day, especially with what I now know, is talk about you constantly. Sarah is that, Sarah is this. Sarah did this today. Half the time I felt that you two were married.'

That was not the answer I was expecting. 'Jealous? Ah, ah, ah. You're kidding. I was the one who was jealous of you. We did everything together. We.'

After all these years, I come to realise one thing. Now I understand why he was jealous of me.

I hold his hand and ask, 'Can you do one thing for me?'

Mark is worried, 'Go on.'

I want one of my wishes completed; 'Promise when I am gone, you will marry Kerry.'

Mark is relieved, 'I thought you were going to make me like you. Promise one thing first.'

I worry now, 'What is that?'

Mark shows no expression, 'You tell Kerry how you really feel. If you don't, you will not find peace when the time comes.'

I give him a slight smile, 'That is the reason why I am taking her with me.'

Mark agrees to marry Kerry and we have reconciliation. Now it is the turn of Mercedes and Natalie.

. . .

MERCEDES FIGHTS BACK the tears as she holds my hands, 'What's it like?'

I do not understand the question, 'How do you mean?'

Mercedes makes herself clear, 'Are you afraid of dying?'

I have thought about this since that day I found out. 'I already believe in a god. Every day, someone is dying of cancer. Why would I be any more special than them? Why would I ask God to keep me alive over everyone else with cancer? If I was to survive, God would have automatically done that. I have led a good life; I have not abused my body, not intentionally hurt anyone, emotionally or physically. So, the answer to your question is no.'

Natalie asks me a question, 'If you had known that this would happen, would you have done anything different?'

I think for a moment, trying to come up with a regret, 'I regret not making time for my private life. I would have liked to have had a child. I would have sacrificed my career to have a family.'

After I have finished talking to Natalie and Mercedes, I ask for some time alone to contact my parents.

DOCTOR CHOPRA COMES to see me to discuss a care package. He assures me that I will be fine with administering my cocktail of drugs. I have no needles to worry about. It is all in a big white paper bag. It has everything I need. Doctor Chopra decides to hug me as he knows this is the last time he will see me. He has a warm hug.

28

THE LONG GOODBYE

I close the curtains to put my clothes back on. Once I am changed and check that I am decent, I pull open the curtain to see Georgina and Freiya. They came back with some coffee. I realise with the commotion, that I have not had a chance to explain.

Ben and Clare arrive flustered. I feel I have lots to say but not enough time. Now Kerry comes back, all flustered, with my things. Ben, Clare, Georgina and Freiya all stare at Kerry and wonder what is going on.

I stare at Kerry and put my hand out to her to let her know I will explain, 'Wow, I am glad you are all here. I called Ben and Clare here as I was hoping I could make proper closure. With everyone.'

Natalie and Mercedes come through the door now, which I am glad of because I would have missed them so much.

Georgina walks over to me and holds my hand. 'It's okay. We are all here now. The floor is yours.' She steps away to allow me to see everyone.

I take turns to talk to each of them for the others to hear. 'Everyone, this is Ben, the one with whom I would have been proud to have children and get married. I never told Ben that I had names if it was a girl or a boy. If it was a girl, Leila and a boy, Luke. Clare, take care of him. He likes his tea fairly weak. He prefers to sleep on the left side of the bed. Georgina and Freiya, I bought you a honeymoon to go and see dolphins. It was going to be a surprise but circumstances have changed. Thank you so much for having me be a part of your life and your wedding.'

Georgina and Freiya struggle to hold the tears back which almost sets me off.

I turn to Natalie and Mercedes, 'You two, I will miss you like hell. I miss the laughs, cries. Especially the laughs.'

I cannot speak anymore as I burst into tears and everyone gathers around me. I really do not want to leave them behind. I wish there was some kind of miracle.

After we stop hugging, Clare personally gives me a hug and promises me that she will take care of Ben. Ben awkwardly gives me a hug and whispers in my ear that he still loves me and that it will take him time to move on. That sets me off again.

Eventually, it just leaves Kerry and I want to tell her something in private, for her ears only and no one else.

WHEN WE GET to Heathrow Airport, we find where my parents are and call their mobiles to find them. When we finally do, I spend time with them to say my final goodbyes. Through the tears, I tell them that I have arranged everything concerning my body. I do not go into detail but put their minds at rest that it is all sorted.

I already purchased the flight as an open-ended ticket and we can go on the next available flight. I want to give my parents and myself that time to properly say goodbye.

WHEN MY PARENTS FINALLY LEAVE, we hand our luggage in and get our boarding passed. We do not go to duty-free. We sit together holding each other's hands and knowing that this is my way of allowing Kerry to say goodbye to me in private. This flight and the brief holiday are to allow for us to have closure; to get out the things we never said to each other when we were growing up and catch up with the past that we let go when she met Mark. Finally, it allows me to thank her for everything she has done in my short life.

DURING THE FLIGHT, a few times, Kerry struggles to get out her words and becomes flustered. I tell her that it is okay. When the time is ready, you will have a chance to tell me.

The flight takes what felt like forever as I start getting anxious about time. Time is suddenly important and precious. Each minute that goes by means a minute less of having Kerry in my life.

WE FINALLY LAND at Los Angeles and take an internal flight to Phoenix Sky Harbour International Airport. I could not find a direct flight. From there, we take a coach transfer to New Mexico, a six-hour drive.

. . .

THE JOURNEY IS TAKING its toll on me but I keep a brave face to hide my condition from Kerry. We can see the sun setting in the distance and it is beautiful. We would not get that kind of view in England.

WE FINALLY REACH our destination in the middle of nowhere. Kerry is so tired and disorientated, wondering where we are. It is night time now and there are no street lights.

Someone comes inside the coach to welcome us and tell us where we are staying. He is American, with a fairly thick accent. I cannot really see what his features are, as we are sat closer to the back. We have been told that we are staying in a plush glamping tent. Kerry asks what we are doing here. I nervously tell her that we are going to fly into space. Kerry's jaw drops and she asks how much that is going to cost her. I tell her that I have already paid for the trip and that it cost £350,000. Kerry's jaw drops again.

WE GET inside our tent and it is like a hotel room. There is proper flooring and makeshift plasterboard walls to create individual rooms. We have a proper bath and shower unit with separate toilet facilities. It is decorated in neutral colours of cream, beige and white. Both of us are shocked by how luxurious it feels. We have separate beds in the same room.

Kerry is absolutely exhausted from the long drive. I know I am close to collapsing but muster the energy to hold it together. Luckily, we had someone carry our bags for us.

Neither of us is in the mood to make conversation. Kerry goes into the shower first and I feel like having a bath. Kerry is happy for both of us to go into the bathroom at the same time. She is insistent in helping me to get into the bath, to make sure I do not fall over. I do not feel awkward with her seeing me naked.

I watch her going into the shower. It is the first time I have seen her naked body and, because of her work, she is very toned with slightly tanned arms from working outside. Her bum is also firm and tight.

I FIND myself drifting in and out of sleep as I hear the sound of the shower. It is like listening to the rain. I feel my second dose of medication wearing off as I start to get a headache. I panic a bit hoping that I do not get another nosebleed. I keep sniffling, worrying that it may not be mucus. It is a weird feeling drifting off to sleep knowing that my head is starting to pound and yet it is not keeping me awake.

I feel my head going underwater, but I seem to be in a euphoric state and it does not scare me. I suddenly feel arms going around me and hear Kerry's voice shouting at me. It startles me and I open my eyes. Kerry lectures me as she tears up.

I feel half asleep, 'What happened?'

Kerry is like a mother to me. 'You started slipping under the water. If we hadn't used the bathroom together, you could have drowned. Do you know how upset I would have been? Gosh, let me get you out.'

I feel guilty, 'Sorry. I am so sorry. I didn't think I was that tired.'

Kerry gradually calms down and starts apologising; 'It is not you. It is just you mean a lot to me. There are so many things I have to say, things that I am scared I will never have a chance to tell you.'

I smile at her. 'It is okay. I am not going yet. Not now.'

She helps me to walk into our bedroom and puts me on my bed. Our eyes lock and we simply stare at each other. After a while, Kerry realises what she is doing and fidgets as she checks I am comfortable. I cannot stop staring at her, thinking that she is sweet for mummying me. Without warning, she drops her towel and stands there with her back to me, stark naked again. She bends over to look inside her suitcase for pyjamas. Her legs are slightly apart as she continues to take out all her items to get to her clothes. She moans to herself why she did not pack her pyjamas last. Once she finds them, she stands up and turns to face me. She takes her time pulling up her trousers. She is not going to wear underwear underneath her bottoms. She notices me watching her and she smiles and asks if I am okay. Once she is ready for bed, she helps me get changed into my pyjamas. Kerry is not fazed at having to change me. Once we are both dressed for bed, I take my cocktail of drugs to ease the pain and then get into bed.

KERRY IS quiet and I glance over to see that we are both facing the ceiling and staring up. She has her hands behind her head. She appears to be deep in thought. I ask if she is okay.

Kerry finally starts to open up; 'There is something that I never told you.'

I ask her to expand. 'Whatever it is, good or bad, it is okay. I am not fragile.'

Kerry is still staring up at the ceiling. 'Mark and I have always argued over you. He even accused me of liking you more than just as a friend.'

I have no idea what she is trying to tell me. 'I don't know what you mean. Did he think I was trying to break you up?'

Kerry scoffs at the notion. 'Sarah, you are really naive. You know that. Nothing is black and white.'

I ask if I have upset her; 'Is there something I did to wrong you? If I have upset you, then I am sorry. For whatever it is.'

Kerry scoffs at me again, 'Do I have to spell it out to you? Mark thinks that we were having a thing. We kept on arguing about it, which is probably why we never married.'

I suddenly feel like laughing. 'You're joking. Come on. Us? How could I possibly be a threat to him? Look at me. I am not exactly god's gift!'

Kerry goes quiet and hesitates to speak, 'Well, you meant something to me. Still do. Will do.'

I stop laughing. 'Well, I became jealous when you met Mark. I felt I lost a really close friend. But I moved on. But never really moved on. Just lived with it.'

Kerry goes on, 'I want to let you know that you never left my thoughts.'

I feel the same way; 'That is why I stopped coming round. You were in my heart. That was enough for me.'

We finish having our heart to heart conversation and eventually switch the side lamp off and go to sleep.

THE NEXT MORNING, I wake up to see that Kerry is not in bed. I get out and walk outside the bedroom to see if she is in the main room. She comes out of the bathroom already changed. She is in a flowery dress that falls down to her knees. It is a tailored, slim fit white dress with a black leaf print. She was hoping to wake me up herself.

I go to get changed. I wear a pair of trouser shorts and a long-sleeved white blouse with single-button cuffs. Kerry tells me that someone came and told her that breakfast is in a separate tent. We both go and see what they have on.

ALL THE OTHER guests are already here and having their food. We find the catering tent is an actual tent. It has a thick black carpet that is woven like a rug. It is crinkled where people have disturbed it with their feet. There is a long table like a boarding school dining hall.

Everyone is quietly eating their food. We have a choice of an English breakfast or continental. We go for continental and with it being so warm outside, have chilled fruit and juice to drink. It is too warm for a hot drink of tea or coffee.

We sit next to each other, somewhere near the middle where there is a gap. Kerry is starting to get excited about going into space. She is a little nervous about the flight but the thought of seeing space overshadows the nerves.

The other guests' accents sound like they are from all over the world. I think I can make out German, Russian and Italian. Once we finish our breakfast, we go back to your tent, very briefly, before having to have an orientation.

· · ·

WE ARE STANDING in the open and the crew, including Richard Branson, are there. They take turns to tell us their names and their backgrounds.

Richard Branson thanks us for coming and tells that he will not be coming on the flight; as part of the experience, we get to meet the man behind the creation of flight into space.

Kerry is more relaxed, now she understands how it works and that the flight will feel like a normal commercial flight. In the background behind them, we can see the plane that will be taking us up.

SOON AFTER THE presentation is finished, we are asked to board the plane. One of the crew calls out my name and I check to see if there is someone else with the same name. When no one else responds, I put my hand up after the second call.

They have supplied me with a wheelchair as a precaution, should I fall ill or not have the energy to keep standing. I forget that I pre-warned them about my health. The wheelchair is already on board but they will make sure that no one else will take it.

ONCE WE ARE INSIDE, it feels quite snug and there is not much room to walk around. They tell us that we will not be floating as the plane is pressurised. They also tell us over the tannoy that when we are close to the Earth's surface, the rocket will kick in to propel us into space. Once we are inside the 'Karman Line', we will orbit the Earth once and then land back down. It will take about an hour and a half to go round the Earth.

When the rocket kicks in, we get pushed back in the chair. The thruster only comes on for about thirty-seconds and we are in space. The pilot tells us over the tannoy that we can now move out of our seats and stare out the windows. The plane has triangular-shaped glass windows rounded off on the corners. There are plenty of windows for each of us to see out of.

Kerry is like a school kid in a sweet shop. She is overwhelmed by Earth's bright pale blue surface. We get to see the Earth go from light to darkness, then back to light. It is strange that we are passing the Earth faster than it is orbiting.

The stars are so crystal clear that it feels like you can reach out and pluck them.

HALFWAY THROUGH THE FLIGHT, I start to feel strange I do not feel any pain as the drugs are still working, but I find myself drifting in and out of consciousness again, like how I was in the bath. However, this is slightly different. My friends appear and they are watching me with tears in their eyes. I have to sit down and tell Kerry that I will be in the wheelchair. But before I can do anything, I collapse in front of Kerry and lie on the floor.

Kerry is startled and quickly crouches down next to me. She rests my head in her lap. I stare up at her and feel that it is time now. There are so many things I still have to say to her. I realise that I love her and I always have loved her. I wish that I knew I fancied her all those years back; we could have found out if we could have had a future. But she is straight and I would not expect her to respond in the same way. Still, I need closure; I need to tell her about my feelings or else it will be too late.

I have already written her a letter but that was before I realised that I love her. The letter is a part of my will.

I feel my soul is floating out of my body but I am still here. My friends are still with me, watching us laying here together.

The gnome seems to know why I am light-headed; 'It is time, Sarah. It is time.'

At first, I do not know what he means until my head starts to hurt, then I say, 'Okay, I am ready. But let me say goodbye to Kerry.'

The gnome smiles through his tears, 'You only have a few minutes. We will see you on the other side.'

Kerry turns to where I am staring and is confused, 'Who are you talking you?'

I smile at her as I gaze into her eyes; 'Only my imaginary friends who I have been talking to since November last year. They are telling me it is time now.'

Kerry begins to panic; 'You cannot. I haven't told you everything that I need to say. I was going to tell you when we get back to our camp.'

I stare at her and insist, 'Tell me now. Before it is too late.'

Kerry's face is going blurry, 'Okay. I am going to miss you like crazy. I don't want you to leave me. If I could trade places, I would. You have led a better life than me. You deserve to live.'

I have to touch her face to know she is still there. 'I have to let you know that I love you. I have always loved you. I understand why I was jealous of Mark.'

Kerry holds my hand against her face; 'I love you too. It is the reason why I have not been bothered whether Mark marries me or not.'

I smile as I feel her smile in my hand. 'I am ready now. I can go now.'

Kerry is not ready, 'No. No. Not now. I have only realised that I love you. I want to feel you. Make love.'

I can see her face again, 'You can feel me. I feel you. I'm not afraid.'

Kerry begs me to stay; 'Please, God, not now. Please let me have more time with her.'

I need to say one more thing; 'I believe that I will be asked one question when I get judged. When they ask me what I did with my life, I'll tell them... I spent it looking... for you.'

KERRY HAS tears flowing down her cheeks when she hears Sarah speak those words. Before she has a chance to respond, the light in Sarah's eyes goes out. Her face relaxes and her eyes do not move. Her body feels lifeless and her hand falls away from her face.

Kerry is hysterical and holds the lifeless body against herself and cries uncontrollably. She thinks by squeezing her against herself, she will come back. She smells her hair and clothes to be reminded of her and feels that she is still here.

People around her walk over and know that it is too late. They know that she needs to spend time holding her best friend and her love interest.

29

TIES THAT BIND

There is a closed coffin on a stretch-wheeled bier, at the front of the church. Sarah's friends and work colleagues, including Belinda and Julie, are there. Sarah's parents are sat at the front not far from where the coffin is centred.

The vicar begins the service and follows the content inside the order of service book. Between the lessons and address by the vicar, there are hymns sung.

Her friends, Natalie, Georgina, Mercedes and finally Kerry each tell how they remember her. They tell a personal story of how they met and how much of a friend Sarah was to them. Kerry finds it the hardest to tell what Sarah really meant to her. She has to lie so that she does not embarrass her partner Mark in front of the congregation.

Finally, Ben walks up and stands in front of everyone. He has an unopened letter that Sarah gave him at the hospital. He was told not to open it until the funeral. Ben speaks up, explaining that he is following the wishes of Sarah, and takes out the letter.

His hands are shaking as he opens it. He scours the letter to see what the content is and see if it will embarrass him or anyone. He then smiles as he likes what is written.

Ben clears his throat and begins, 'This letter is for her parents and any friends who feel they were touched by her short life. Here goes.'

"There are no rules or instructions on how to react or behave. The seconds of breakthrough you feel are a relief for your loss. I am no longer in pain. I lived a good life and I have my parents to thank for that. I no longer feel a burden to my parents, Ben or friends, even though that is my perception.

In the same moment you are missing me terribly, the most important thing is that you were with me constantly. We cherished every moment together and so I have no regrets. So, you should have no guilt whatsoever. Don't put a time or deadline on grieving."

BEN'S VOICE quivers and he struggles to finish the letter. Clare's knee-jerk reaction is to stand by him and finish the letter. They both hold either side of the letter and she continues.

"IT COULD LAST A VERY long time. So, cope with it, don't fight it. You both have each other and better. Laugh at the comments I made as they are as important as grieving. You will see me again when it is your time. I am not lost forever. I am only in a different place. Don't fight the tears. Let them flow out. It shows compassion for your loss. Don't feel guilty for having a fun moment as that is what I would want. So, goodbye for now, but not forever."

THE CHURCH IS quiet and you can hear a pin drop.

A FEW DAYS LATER, Sarah's wishes are carried out by Ben firm.Mercedes receives money to pay for her IVF, enough for three attempts. She is open mouthed when she opens the post and almost faints. Her and her husband are tearful.

Sarah's parents mortgage is cleared. She also donates some money towards doctor Chopra research which leaves him overwhelmed.

NINE MONTHS LATER.

GEORGINA AND FREIYA have recently had their first child and are at home ready to go for a drive. They have made a promise to someone special. They name their baby Luke as promised.

They pack their car with Luke's changing bag, some toys gifted to them and a baby blanket bought by the donor.

They head off to see parents. They drive for twenty minutes across Milton Keynes.

.   .   .

WHEN THEY ARRIVE, they spend time searching for a space to park. They then get their baby out of the car and Freiya carries his car seat on her arm. Then they knock on the door and glance at each other in excitement.

When the door opens, it is Sarah's dad who opens the door. Georgina is proud to introduce Luke to his grandparent. Sarah's dad is confused when he peers at their baby and wonders why he is called a granddad. Freiya explains that one of the gifts Sarah gave before she died was to donate her eggs to them so they could have a child. In return, they were asked to have Sarah's parents involved as Luke's grandparents as well as Georgina and Freiya's parents.

Sarah's dad breaks down in tears and waits for permission to take him out of the car seat.

They both nod in excitement and he holds him in his arms. Sarah's mum comes to the door wondering why he is taking so long. Sarah's dad stares at Sarah's mum through his joyful tears and tells her that they have a grandchild.

PLEASE LEAVE A REVIEW!

To The Stars

Thank you so much for buying and reading my book!!

This is my fifth novel that I have written.

I have drawn from my own experiences to create my characters. They are not based on friends or family of real persons; apart from myself and fictional plot.

I mulled over the idea of writing my first novel, Jane Knight Rogue Officer, in August 2016. I then found the courage to begin my first novel in December 2016. I did not finish my novel until March 2018. My wife and I became a family in June 2017. This postponed completing my first novel.

My first genuine review for this book was not until May 2020. I value my readers reviews because I then know they completed my book. Not half completed and never picked up again.

I plan on becoming a full time author by building up my catalogue of various genres that focus on Steamy, Hot & Passionate themes whether Romance, Action & Adventure or Thrillers.

BOOKS ALSO BY LEON M A EDWARDS

Please visit the following links to these books

Leon M A Edwards Amazon Author Page

Leon M A Edwards Author Website

LEON M A EDWARDS CLUB

Join my Leon M A Edwards Club to receive future free ebook copies before release date.

I like to send out my books before I publish to hear peoples opinions.

Subscribe

The link above will take you to the subscription page.

COPYRIGHT

Printed in Great Britain
by Amazon